CALLED

CALLED

SOUTHERN WATCH
BOOK ONE

Robert J. Crane

CALLED
SOUTHERN WATCH
BOOK ONE

1st Edition

AUTHOR'S NOTE
This book is a work of fiction. Names, characters, places and incidents are products of the author's imagination or are used fictitiously. Any resemblance to actual events or locales or persons, living or dead, is entirely coincidental.

Layout provided by Everything Indie
http://www.everything-indie.com

Acknowledgments

These were the people who helped me launch this new series:

Shannon Garza, who signed on with enthusiasm to assist in the beginning, when all I had was a mission statement. Thanks for believing in me, Red.

Carien Keevey, who watched Justified before reading this and didn't draw but maybe one comparison between my boy Hendricks and Raylan Givens. I'm sure reading this southern-ish dialcct stuff wasn't easy for her, but she made it through somehow.

Heather Rodefer was buried under mountains of things to edit and real-life emergencies, yet still found time to get through this for me, and for that I am grateful. She's always my beta editor-in-chief.

Jerod Heck gave me a read-through that included everything I needed to make sure Hendricks sounded like a real Marine, not a lazy writer behind a desk. Much thanks, dude. I'll have a Leinie's in your honor later. (Bwahahaha!)

David Leach took an early look at the manuscript and made sure I didn't eff things up too bad. David's been a great sounding board on this and the Sanctuary Series, and to him I owe great thanks.

My Uncle Larry and Aunt Rita let me bring one of my kids down to spend time on their farm while I started the first draft of this manuscript. Thanks to them I got a ridiculous amount of writing done while still having a lot of fun.

My Grandparents also let me come to visit them to write part of this, while bringing my same pre-schooler destruction crew with me, and I similarly got a lot done. Thanks to them for the help.

Sarah Barbour has got to be one of the longest-suffering souls in this business. She gets to see the mess of my manuscripts after I've already rejected an abundant number of changes from my beta readers. She gets through them with a steely eye toward the details, though, and I'm always amazed at the things she catches. Also, she recommended I describe Hendricks's coat as a "duster," figuring you'd all know what that means, but

I totally rejected that change. Google "drover coat," you'll be fine.

My thanks as always to Karri Klawiter for her efforts on the cover, as always. She's such a joy to work with.

To my parents, especially, who accompanied me during much of my travels while writing this book so they could provide babysitting, and to my wife who remained at home to manage the fort, I owe my thanks. Also, to my kids, for making sure I have a little fun every day.

Chapter 1

He came to town riding the wind; when he left, he reckoned he'd do it just about the same way. The thing was, Lafayette Jackson Hendricks had been in the wind a long damned time, and he'd had just about enough of that shit to last a lifetime. In his current occupation, though, that life expectancy was not terribly long compared to most. But that was nothing new. It never had been, not in either of the occupations he'd chosen in his life.

He reflected on all this as he stepped off the running board of the big Mack truck, the engine brake squealing as he jumped down, an old Marine duffel slung over his back, the strap running over his long black drover coat. It was summer, it was night, and it was raining. The drover coat was a duster that helped keep the rain off him. The black cowboy hat he wore helped even more, but it was still coming down bad enough that his jeans were soaked at the bottom almost as soon as his boots hit the ground. The boots were old and leather and faded from landing in puddles just like this all over the U.S.

Hendricks could hear the subtle click of his heels against the blacktop over the rain as it started to slacken up a little. The semi that had carried him pulled down the ramp back onto the interstate, rumbling out of sight. He pulled up the sleeve of his coat to take a peek at his watch. It was just after ten o'clock.

The smell of the rain was fresh, but the heat was pervasive, even at this time of night, making the rain seem like a warm shower. It was summer, after all, and damned humid, something even the downpour hadn't been able to alleviate. The taste of dinner from the restaurant where he'd met the trucker who had given him the ride was still lingering on Hendricks's tongue, and he'd forgotten to buy a pack of gum to replace the one he'd finished somewhere in Kentucky. The mint was sorely missed right now, and he rubbed his tongue uncomfortably against the top of his mouth.

His boots clicked against the pavement, carrying him ahead, and the headlights of a passing car caught a green sign in the distance just enough for him to see it even in the dark of the Tennessee night.

Entering Calhoun County.

*

Archibald “Arch” Stan turned his patrol car around just before the county line, his headlights illuminating a figure walking along the side of the road. It was a guy, a duffel on his back and a black cowboy hat and drover coat keeping the rain off him. The rain was letting up, at least to Arch’s eyes, after a deuce of a downpour only a few minutes earlier. A real frog-strangler, his mother would have said. Gully washer, he’d have called it. In either case, he felt bad for the cowboy who was in it now. He started to pull over to say something to the guy when his radio crackled to life.

“Fifteen, this is Dispatch, come back.”

He hesitated for only a second and he thumbed the mike. “Fifteen here, go ahead.”

“Fifteen, sheriff asks that you return to the station.”

Arch felt a faint swirl of amusement before he clicked the mike on again. “I know, I know, I’m getting perilously close to overtime.”

He could hear laughter in the voice of the dispatcher at the other end of the radio, Erin Harris. “You know the boss likes to pinch those pennies until he can hear Abe Lincoln scream as they're leaving his hand.”

Arch sighed. “Tell him I’ll be clocking out in five. Wouldn’t want to make hard work a habit around here, after all.”

“Damned right. Save that crap for when you’re off the clock,” Harris said, her drawl especially conspicuous over the radio. “Channel it into making your wife happy around the house; it’ll do you more good than trying to bleed overtime dollars out of—” There was a subtle hiss as Harris paused, and when she came back on her tone was more formal. “Uh, we’ll see you in five, Fifteen. Dispatch out.”

Arch grinned. No doubt the sheriff had just popped his head out of his office. “Right you are, Dispatch. Over and out.”

He had been driving steadily the entire time he’d been talking, the black surface of County Highway 12 carrying him east, back toward the town of Midian. He was less than a mile away now, and he gave one last glance behind him to the figure walking along the side of the road. The guy had probably been let off at the interstate bridge by a trucker and was headed toward Midian or parts beyond. Any other quiet night, Arch might have had him get in the back, behind the security grill that kept him separated from arrestees, and given the guy a ride to town. The rain spotted his windshield as he drove, and the faint lights of Midian were just ahead, over the hill. He sighed and watched the drifter disappear behind him as he went down into a dip in the road. No room in the budget for being a nice guy, not in this economy, anyway. He was lucky to still have a law enforcement job, especially in Calhoun County.

"Good luck, Cowboy," he whispered and put the pedal down on the accelerator. He had to be back at the station in less than five minutes, after all.

*

They called him Hollywood when they thought he wasn't listening. For the locals, "the city" meant Chattanooga, or Knoxville, maybe Atlanta, the small town hicks. No, when the man they called Hollywood said "the city," they figured out pretty quickly he was talking about L.A., and his nickname, well, it came pretty shortly after.

In their culture—not southern culture, but their true one, the demon culture—names were power, so you didn't exchange names, and you damned fucking sure didn't ask for one, not until one was offered to you. Even these hicks knew better than that, and for just that little bit of etiquette, Hollywood was grateful.

He'd hired four of them, flashing a wad of cash around and doling it out a little at a time. The first hundred was a good start, and the roll he'd carried promised more if he was kept happy with their services. They were all small time, not used to people from Atlanta coming through, he figured, let alone some big-shot big shit from L.A. They all kind of marveled at it, marveled at him, deferred to him. And why shouldn't they? He was gonna be paying the bills, after all.

"I love it," Hollywood whispered. He pushed the ponytail off his shoulder, feeling the smooth texture of his pricey suit. The rain had stopped, thankfully, and the quiet of the night was punctuated by the occasional sound of dripping, water making its way down the drainpipes of the metal barn not fifteen feet from where he was standing.

They were just inside a fence, one that the four of them had opened for him, stepping and fetching like he was some kind of royalty. In reality, he was the man with money, which made him royalty around here. Calhoun County offered damned little work for their kind, Hollywood suspected. A patron for them was probably something long-desired. One that drew water like he did … well, that was a bonus, surely. "Seriously," Hollywood breathed. "I love it."

One of them had the balls to say it. "Umm … it's a fucking cow pasture, man." He quieted down after that, though.

It was a cow pasture. A few acres of fenced-in ground, green in the daylight but barely visible in the night. The smell of manure wafted faintly, suppressed by the recent rain but still there and pungent. The night air was stifling. The rain hadn't eased the humidity at all; it had just trapped it there, like a prisoner awaiting a release that wasn't coming anytime soon. It was the sort of shit that caused even Hollywood to sweat, and he wasn't the kind to sweat easily.

"You know what your problem is?" Hollywood said after a moment's silence. His Gucci loafers squished in the wet grass. Squished. He grimaced inside, but actor that he was, didn't let it show. "You lack vision," he told his enthusiastically waiting audience. These backwoods hicks hung on his every word. And why wouldn't they? "Exterior—night!" He said, walking forward slowly, almost stalking, his hands held out in front of him forming a square with his fingers and thumbs, as though he were filming something. "A group of demons prepare to bring forth an ancient evil, one that will consume the entirety of the world, ridding it of the plague of those fucking humans—" He said it like a curse, meant it like a curse, like he was talking about the vilest thing ever made, which he was, "—and restore it to the righteous, tipping the scales and …" He stopped and looked back at the four of them, these sad-sack locals, these meth-taking hillbillies who probably didn't even make enough in a lifetime to afford one Gucci loafer, let alone a pair. "You're not seeing it, are you?"

There was a pause before the answer, the same ballsy one as before. "It's a cow pasture, man. You just stepped in a pie."

"A … pie?" Hollywood hesitated, then the smell hit him and he felt a little ooze in the shoe. He forced a smile. Acting. He should have been an actor; he would have been genius at it. "Local flavor. That's what that is." He inhaled deeply through his nose and regretted it. "Whatever." He shrugged it off, then opened his eyes and looked for the one with the flannel shirt that was cut off at the shoulders. "You. Bring me my book."

It took the local just a second to react, then he came running forward with the book, a heavy, leather-bound tome that was absolutely unlike anything they made nowadays. It wasn't cheap or flimsy. It was … it was like organic produce, dammit, not the factory shit you picked up in the big-box bookstores. Hollywood took it, felt the weight of it in his hands, and opened it up. "It's probably too much to hope for that any of you boys speak Latin, isn't it?" He looked at the semi-circle still standing back and then at the one closest to him. "Never mind." He put on his best ingratiating smile. "Now … where's the farmer?" There was a pause from the little circle, and he waited for the answer. It didn't come. "Where's the fucking farmer?" Hollywood asked again, this time annoyed. Stupid hicks.

"In his house?" came the suggestion a moment later.

"Well, FOR FUCK'S SAKE!" Hollywood said, finally letting out a little of the anger he'd been holding back. It was good to let it out, let these losers see something beneath the veneer. Maybe that was the kind of management style they related to, something more emotion-based. "I said we'd need the farmer, didn't I?" He thought about hitting the sleeveless wonder who'd handed him the book, because, hey, he was closest, but he decided against it. That was for later. It would probably have to happen eventually, just to let them know not to fuck with him, but it didn't have to happen yet. They were probably like dogs and could be yelled into better results. "Go get the farmer." He paused as three of them made to turn around. "You," he said to the one in the sleeveless flannel shirt, "you stay with me." He lowered his voice, talking to himself, the only intelligent one here. "I said we'd need the famer, didn't I? Did I not say it? For fuck's sake."

"Uh huh," the sleeveless one said, "you did."

"Wasn't talking to you."

After a moment's silence, after the footsteps of the other three had a chance to fade, Sleeveless turned to him again. "So … are we making a movie here?"

Hollywood stared at him like he was the dumbest fuck to walk the face of the earth. "Hell, no. I'd never hire you to shoot a movie." He paused. "You're non-union."

The other boys came back a few minutes later, hustling along in the dark. He could see them coming and turned away. It was better not to look at them right now, not let them think he was reliant on them, or that he approved of them in any way. That would be for later, if they managed to do this next bit without screwing up. This shit coming up was for all the marbles, after all.

"Uh, Hollywood?" one of them started off as he approached, and Hollywood turned back to see there were five of them coming, his three boys and two more being shoved along in front of them. "He had his wife there with him …" He wanted to sigh but didn't because this was actually good. Better two than one, right?

"Fine, fine," Hollywood said. Better not to give them too much encouragement, but he also didn't want them to miss this important lesson. "Good initiative. Better to have her here than not." The lone lamp hanging off the barn revealed the two new folks as they got closer. He gave them only the barest moment's study and took in old, lined faces. Old was really all he saw. "This'll do." He turned away from them and looked back, back to the pasture, where a— *something* had wandered right into the middle of the field since last he'd looked. "Is that—" He squinted. "Is there a fucking *cow* in the middle of my fucking ritual?"

"No," said the farmer in a southern accent, "but there's one in the middle of my goddamned cow pasture, you Yankee jackass!"

Hollywood blinked after looking at the animal then turned back to the ballsy farmer and smiled his fake, laying-on-the-bullshit-with-a-shovel smile. It had helped him seal a few deals. "I like the energy that you're bringing to this. You've got real personality." Hollywood took a step closer and put an arm around the farmer's shoulder. The man's hands were restrained by one of the demons, and it looked like the enthusiasm might have wrenched the old man's shoulder out of joint. That was good, too, so far as Hollywood was concerned. "I bet you tried to fight these boys off," he said, gesturing at his new employees.

"Damned right," the farmer said through gritted teeth. He looked ready to spit at Hollywood.

"He went for a shotgun," one of the lessers said, a dark-haired, mustached fellow with a Metallica t-shirt on. "He almost lost the arm for that one."

"Shotgun wouldn't do much on these boys," Hollywood said, tightening his grasp around the farmer's shoulders. "But I admire your spirit." He grinned, and the shovel got bigger. "Really, I do. I admire it so much … that I'm going to sacrifice it."

"Beg pardon?" the farmer said with an air of disbelief. The man smelled of cowshit.

Hollywood withdrew his arm and the smell came with it. It was in the air, all around, but he knew—just knew—that it was on his suitcoat now, like it was seeping into his pores. He shook his head in disbelief before he caught hold of himself and restored the grin, the image—the acting—and put the ingratiating smile back on. "So …" he gestured to the cow that had wandered into the middle of the field. "… does the cow have a name, or are they all just thoughtless beasts to you?"

"Her name's Creampuff," the farmer said after a moment's pause and a look at the men surrounding him.

"Really?" Hollywood said. "Creampuff? Do you hate it or something?" This elicited a laugh from the new employees, but the farmer started to say something. "Doesn't matter, don't answer. Time?" he asked the sleeveless one again.

"Uh …" He didn't have a watch, the sleeveless one, but he managed to shuffle the book around to one hand and pull out his cell phone. The screen flared and lit up the angular lines of his face. "11:59."

"Right," Hollywood said, and clapped his hands together. "Let's get this underway, shall we?" He wanted to pick his teeth, to take a shower—preferably in blood, but water would help, too—to get this stink off him. But there were certain sacrifices that one had to make to gain power, to be a broker, to bring about BIG THINGS.

And he was all for bringing about BIG THINGS. The biggest, really.

"Normally, I'd have some of you chanting in Latin for background noise," he said as he strode back over to the sleeveless one, "but that's just because it was the way I came up on these rituals, not because it's important. All that really matters are the key components." He pointed his thumbs delicately toward himself, "The vessel," he pointed toward the book, "the words," and finally he pointed toward the farmer, who was looking at the whole scene as though he was about ready to make good on spitting in Hollywood's face, though that wouldn't do much for anyone, least of all the farmer, "and finally the sacrifice." He halted for a second. "Sacrifices, if necessary."

He waited and wondered what he was waiting for. Approval? Hah. Not from these hicks. Never. They were so far beneath him as to not even register. He gave a sort of shrug, entirely to himself and which only he understood, dismissing them all, and turned to the book which one of the fleas he had hired was holding out for him.

The words that came out next were probably entirely perplexing to the farmer and his wife and not understood even by any of his four employees, but again, who cared? Not him. He understood every word of the language, because it was his first. Besides, it hadn't been spoken on earth in millennia. And certainly not conversationally, even then.

"*Vecede en shi, vecede en barten, urgan ves pui, urgan ves porsace.*" He let his mind do the translating, "I beckon you forward from the nether realms, O Mighty, and seek to join my form to yours. I call you forth from the darker regions, to the rock of Earth, call you up from the depths to become one with me, to join your dark purpose to mine, and sacrifice this mortal in your name."

With that, he covered the distance between himself and the farmer in an eyeblink, as fast as his feet could carry him, and he took the farmer's throat in his hands. He squeezed, just a gentle little bit for him but strong enough that it broke the farmer's skin, the veins just below the surface. The rush of blood sprayed forth, right in his face. It should have been a relief from the smell of cow shit, but it wasn't, sadly. It was as though everything in this forsaken place was tainted by it. He said the name *Ygrusibas* as he tore into the farmer's throat then waited, waited with the blood on his hands and face and suit as the farmer gurgled his last and was dropped to the muddy, grassy ground next to the boys. Hollywood's boys. He liked that name they'd come up with for him; it fit everything he'd come to align himself with over the last fifty or so years. It was a good image. He took a breath, and he waited.

He waited, and waited, and the earth did not shake, the mountains around him did not burst forth with torrents of fire. The ground did not erupt with all the flames and cold of hell. The smell of cow shit pervaded the air and things remained just about like they'd always been. He didn't really expect any of those things to happen, but it damned sure would have been nice. Any sign would have been nice. Instead, cold, stark silence. And the smell of cow shit.

"Fuck," Hollywood said.

"Did you … read it wrong?" Sleeveless asked. Hollywood shot Sleeveless a look that told him he was going to be changing his name to Ball-less soon enough, and that was the last that was said for a piece. Hollywood walked back to him, read the ritual again—AGAIN—out loud, said the words, same tone, same cadence—same fucking words he'd spoken for thousands of years, he knew how to fucking read them, stupid fucking hillbilly trash questioning him like that. Then he crushed the farmer's wife's throat and made sure she bled on him, because the blood of the sacrifice was key to bringing forth Ygrusibas and always had been. He waited again, this time for a minute, then two.

"Fuck," he cursed again quietly. "Fuck, shit, fuck." This time, none of his boys said anything. They damned well learned quick, for stupid hillbillies. "Get out your cell phone," he told Sleeveless and had him hold it over the book. He read the words again, this time not trusting his memory and the dim light. The words were the same, the exact same as they had been. Exactly what he'd read. He cursed again. Still, his boys said nothing. At least there was that. He flipped to the page before, the page after. Nothing new, nothing unexpected. The words were terse, some obscure, some annoyingly so, since Hollywood had been on earth a damned long time. Too damned long, actually. "Am I losing it in my old age?" he whispered out loud.

"Naw," Sleeveless said.

"Wasn't looking for audience participation, dumbass," Hollywood snapped at him, and Sleeveless took the hint. Good dog. He let his fingers rest on his mouth, his chin, and he tried to contemplate, but nothing was coming to him. He was a problem solver, a fixer, a *producer*, for fuck's sake! "All right, okay. The timing was off, maybe? The day, maybe? Whatever. This isn't that time sensitive. We'll try again tomorrow. And the next day, and the next, and however many days it takes to get it right. This was just a rehearsal."

He looked over the boys, still standing over the fallen bodies of the farmer and his wife. "You got people in this town, right? In this county?" He looked off at the horizon, which was dominated by hills. The locals called them mountains, but Hollywood had been in the High Sierras once, on location. These were hills. Not even a lick of snow. "We'll need a couple more tomorrow night. Maybe three, just to be safe. And we'll keep going, keep going until I crack it. Shouldn't take long, I probably mispronounced something. I'll study it up, make sure I do it right next time." He looked at the corpses in the mud and gestured to them. "I know you'd probably prefer fresh, but … y'know, take what you can get and all that …"

The four of them, his boys, his employees, fell on the bodies, ripping and tearing the flesh. They may have looked human, those boys, but he had known they weren't when he came into town. He could smell them, could smell them a mile off. There was a sort of connection between their kind, the ability to see beyond, to see the signs of each other's passage. He'd sniffed them out, followed their signs back to their trailer, caught them all doing meth. It passed the time, he supposed. Hollywood preferred pot, to stimulate the creative juices, but hey, he didn't begrudge his fellows their vices. He watched the boys rip into the farmer and his wife and frowned. Even if it was flesh that probably tasted of cowshit.

*

Creampuff watched the demons devour the farmer and his wife, dimly aware that they had been the ones that had fed her before, kept her, had cleaned out her pen. It was a messy business, what they were doing to Creampuff's former master, but something else told her it was wholly natural, demons feeding on the flesh of humans. The voice that was speaking to her was unusual, as Creampuff was just a Jersey cow, though she didn't know it. She'd heard the farmer say it, but it didn't matter enough to her to be worth remembering. It mattered now just a little, though, because the new voice was talking, wanting to know what she was, what she was doing, why she had called him forth. The voice had the run of her brain, though, and figured things out pretty quickly. Certainly more quickly than the simple Jersey cow who had been named Creampuff by a man who was presently having his flesh stripped off him by four men who were not men at all. But that was all right, too, Creampuff was told by the voice. The voice that was in her ear, in her body, in her heart and even her very soul, to the extent she had such a thing. It told her all these things, all these things and more, before it realized that it was talking to a cow and decided to just start trying to steer for itself. But for a while, it was a very civil conversation. She was told many, many things, including a name, the name of the voice in her head.

Ygrusibas.

Chapter 2

Arch parked his police cruiser, a big Ford Explorer with sheriff's office markings, in the lot behind the station, a big old brick building that had been built in 1942. It was flat and square, with that age-stained brick that was so common on local government buildings in this part of Tennessee. It had air conditioning which had been put in in the eighties and probably hadn't ever worked right. The walk through the rain-dampened lot was short. Arch pulled open the big Plexiglass door to the station without giving it much thought. It was armored, a concession to the fact that modern law enforcement dealt with risks that hadn't been much of a worry back when the building had been built. The times were changing, even in rural Calhoun County, Tennessee, and in ways that the first occupants of the building would probably not have wanted to have to deal with.

Arch saw his way through the second door and felt the stale air of the station coursing around him as he walked in. The air was just as humid inside but maybe a degree or two cooler. Arch suspected that was due more to it being under the shadow of the roof all day than to with the ineffectual air conditioner.

"Hey, Arch," Erin said from behind the desk as he navigated his way around the waist-high wooden gate that separated the waiting area from the official space behind the counter. "You made it with a minute to spare."

"Yep." Arch slid back around a desk to where the time clock sat, an old, ugly thing that might have been installed at the same time as the building was built, and slid his card out before punching it into the designated slot. "And here I was hoping for a bounteous harvest of overtime with which to support my not-yet burgeoning family."

"More like support your wife in the manner in which she was raised." The voice was warm but carried the faint prickle of familiarity and truth that Arch had come to expect from the sheriff. He turned and caught the wry smile of the balding man standing at the entrance to his office, arms folded as he watched his employees banter back and forth. "I trust your patrol was in line with what we've come to expect of our glorious careers in Calhoun County law enforcement?"

"Pretty boring, yeah," Arch said, putting his time card back where it belonged. "If I'd wanted to liven things up, though, I would have tried for a job in Chattanooga or Knoxville."

"Out there in the big, bad world?" Erin said with a laugh. She was cute, all the guys said so—blond, barely out of high school, spent as much time in the gym as she did in the bar. Which was considerable. She mostly worked dispatch, though Arch had heard her say she wanted to be on patrol. That was harder to come by now, though, with the budget cuts.

"I've never even heard of those places," Sheriff Reeve said, scratching his chin.

"You wouldn't have," Arch said, dutifully playing the straight man and foil to set up the sheriff's wry delivery. "They are outside of Calhoun County, after all."

"There's no such thing," Reeve said with a straight face. "Didn't you hear? The world ends outside the county line. Just drops straight off and down into infinite nothingness."

"You know, boss," Erin said, "you take flat-earthing to a new level."

"I'll assume that's a compliment," Reeve said with a sort of satisfaction. "There's something to be said for being a little mule-headed, after all."

"You mean a stubborn-ass?" Erin said with a muffled laugh.

"I call it uncompromising," Reeve said. "Sounds better to my ears."

"Yeah, well, I call it a long day." Arch rubbed at his eyes.

"I thought you said it was boring?" Reeve let off a hint of interest at this.

"It was," Arch said with a grin. "That's the hardest day of all. I wouldn't mind a little action."

"Not gonna find that in Midian," Erin said, "and probably not much of it in Calhoun, period. What are you gonna run up against? Some old moonshiner making a break from his still? Some idiot blowing up his meth lab? Or some addict strolling naked down Main Street?"

"All I ask is a little excitement," Arch said with a weary smile. "Something to liven up the dull days."

"You best be careful what you wish for," Reeve said with a smile of his own. The man was a thirty-year veteran of law enforcement and knew what he was talking about, Arch knew. "You might find yourself wishing differently shortly thereafter."

"If you want some excitement," Erin said, opening her drawer and grabbing her purse, "I'm meeting Wade and Harlan down at Fast Freddie's for a few beers. That'd liven up your night."

"I wished for more exciting days," Arch said with a smile directed at Erin. "The missus keeps my nights about as lively as I can presently manage."

"Listen to that college-educated gentleman and his fancy understatement," Reeve said with a chuckle. "That's about the most candy-assed way I ever heard a newlywed talk about how much he's getting laid."

Arch let his smile tighten. He wouldn't have said it like that, not ever, but he was getting used to Reeve doing it. The man didn't mean anything by it; it was just the way he talked. Time was, Sheriff Nicholas Reeve could just about blow the smile off Arch's face with minimal effort. The job interview had consisted of a steady stream of profanities, something Arch hadn't much dealt with until he had started playing football. Now he was used to it, but he'd still been a little surprised when he encountered it in a job interview. He shouldn't have been, though; Reeve operated the Sheriff's Department pretty close to how a football coach ran a locker room. There wasn't much room for squeamishness. He glanced toward Erin, who was too busy locking up her drawer to even look up. What might have been called a hostile working environment in a big-city department was just the norm in Calhoun County. Arch expected Reeve had probably screened someone like Erin before hiring her to make sure she wasn't the sort to find offense in much of anything. Which was fortunate.

"Don't even have nothing to say to that?" Reeve asked with a smile of his own. "You just gonna sit there with that shit-eating grin, aren't you? I don't blame you. I was newly married once myself, though I barely remember it. You could at least make a show of trying to give an old man a thrill by letting him live vicariously, though." Reeve wasn't exactly old, only in his mid-fifties, but the time sitting in the car and behind a desk had caught up with him. He wasn't enormous like some of the older lawmen Arch had met, but he was a little soggier around the waist than Arch would have been comfortable being. He still managed to look like a starched lawman in his khaki uniform, though, with his big old revolver on his belt.

"Maybe talk to Harris about that," Arch said finally, nodding at Erin. "She's a barfly, probably has more exciting stories to tell than I do."

"Who, me?" Erin said, looking up in surprise. "Nah, I ain't got nothing interesting going on, not for a while. If I did, I wouldn't be hanging out in Fast Freddie's every night." She gave off a smile that showed her perfectly even teeth. "Besides, you know there ain't nothing worth having in this town ain't already been gotten. Bought and paid for," she pointed to the ring on Arch's finger. "Speaking of which, you best run along; you know if you're even five minutes late, your missus starts calling the station wondering where you're at."

"Sure enough," Reeve said, but the way he said it came out "sho 'nuff." He drawled with the best of them. "Y'all have a good night."

"I'll walk with you," Erin said as Arch rounded the counter on the way back out to his cruiser. The department had gotten the new Explorer before the budget cutbacks. It was the only new vehicle they'd purchased in the last five years, and Arch suspected it had pained Reeve more than a little to pass it off to the most junior patrolman. He'd done it, though, for reasons that Arch didn't want to delve too deeply into.

"You sure you don't want to come with me to Fast Freddie's?" Harris asked again as they split, Arch heading to his Explorer and she to her little subcompact. Being on dispatch and not patrol, Erin drove her own car. "Maybe give Alison a call and take her out for a night on the town?"

"We're not much for drinking, you know," Arch said, rubbing his hand over his stubbled head. He kept it pretty close to buzzed, as much for the convenience as for the regulation way it looked. Most people could tell he was a lawman just by looking at him, even when he was off duty—and that was even if the entire county hadn't already known him. He worked hard to cultivate that image, though, to try to take away that familiarity that everyone presumed because he had been a local legend on the football field. "I doubt the missus is going to be much in the mood to go out after a long day on her feet at Rogerson's." Rogerson's was the grocery store where she worked as an assistant manager. And hated it. And complained about it, every day, at length, to Arch. It was, however, a family business, and certain things were simply expected.

"All right, then," Erin said, slipping into her car seat and giving him a last wave. "If you change your mind, you know where to find us."

"I won't," Arch said tightly, "but thanks." He got in and shut his door, turned the key and listened to the rumble of the engine. The Explorer was a damned sight better than anything he would have been able to afford on his own, that was certain. He shifted it into reverse and slid out of the spot before Erin had a chance to even start her car. It was better this way; as wild as the girl surely was at the bar—and he had heard the tales from his co-workers—she was grandma-slow as a driver.

Arch guided the car out of the parking lot, keeping to the lot limit even though almost no one else did, and turned right on the Old Jackson Highway, County Road 57. It was the main street that ran right through the middle of Midian, and it wasn't but five or so minutes' drive to his apartment. He took a deep breath as he waited for a semi to pass. He rubbed his eyes, let his fingers massage down his face as the big tractor trailer blew past on the rain-slicked street, the new-car smell thick in his nose as he thought for just a second about cutting his lights on and going after it. It was at least seven mph over, and he wrote tickets for less. But he was clocked out, Alison was expecting him, and he'd written tickets all day. It was all he did, write tickets and cite for broken taillights.

"Is that all there is?" he asked the empty car, the turn signal clicking over and over again, tapping gently into his skull. The same boring day, over and over again, every day from now to retirement in some thirty or forty years.

When there was no answer, he went ahead and turned, leaving Erin's lights behind him as she made the right to Fast Freddie's. He, on the other hand, took the left, toward home, the unanswered question still hanging in the air.

*

Hendricks had met a man in the town square who wasn't a man at all. He'd gone to ask a guy wearing a John Deere hat for directions to a cheap hotel, figuring he'd find a place to crash for the night before trying to get the lay of the town tomorrow, and it became real obvious, real fast—at least to his practiced eye—that he was looking at a demon. It had taken some practice, but he could recognize a fair number of them by the signs, and when he saw the little flare of light in the man's eyes, he knew. Worse than that was that the demon seemed to know he'd been spotted because instead of answering with polite directions to the nearest hotel, he instead let show his teeth—the real ones, the demon ones, hiding beneath the veneer of human flesh and skin that the demon wore like Hendricks wore his drover coat.

"Well, shit," Hendricks said as he took a step back. The demon's eyes were positively glowing now, his anger at being found out rising quickly. Green hat, glowing red eyes, well, hell, what else would you find in Midian, Tennessee on a Tuesday night? He didn't wait to have the man-who-was-not-a-man set upon him; he recognized the signs for what they were—the demon, straight from the nether realms, was about to make a meal out of him. No, that wasn't what Hendricks had planned for his Tuesday night in Midian, hell no it wasn't. And like any reasonable demon-hunting individual would, he had a response.

He threw the duffel off his shoulders, drew the sword that was hiding under his drover coat, and braced himself for the literal hell that was about to come his way.

*

Arch had to blink as he passed the square in front of the county courthouse. It was a simple enough square, just like you'd find in any small town, with businesses closed down at this time of night. The whole town rolled up the sidewalks, as he'd heard it said, round about eight o'clock, except for the twenty-four-hour Wal-Mart down by the interstate. Downtown got quiet after eight, and it stayed quiet until the next morning. Kids didn't play there because there was nothing to do. There'd been some vandalism a year ago at the hardware store, a dilapidated old building that had lost a front window, in all probability to some bored high school kid. That sort of thing was big news in Midian. Mostly the square was quiet at night.

So it was with some surprise that when Arch drove through on his way home he saw the man in the black cowboy hat and long black drover coat who he'd passed out by the interstate waving a sword at one of the local boys who worked down at the paper mill. Arch couldn't rightly recollect the ol' boy's name, not off the top of his head, but he knew him, a fellow who had come to town a few years earlier from Athens or Sweetwater or somewhere closer to Knoxville. He was wearing the same John Deere hat he wore most of the time, and he looked like he was telling the cowboy to step off, fire in his eyes.

Arch didn't even think about it, just jerked the Explorer into a parking space at an angle by the square, and was out of his car in a heartbeat, drawing his Glock 22 as he went. "Hands above your head!" he called to the cowboy as he made his way across the pavement toward the middle of the square, which was bisected with an X of concrete walkways that met at a statue of General Stonewall Jackson. "Drop the sword!"

"That'd be a real bad idea right now," the cowboy said, but he froze, the sword high above his head, not like he'd been holding it a minute ago, ready to strike. "This is a Chu'ala—" Arch squinted at the cowboy as the man said some nonsense word, and the next part of the statement jumped clear off the track, "—and its blood lust is about to kick in."

"Drop the sword, sir," Arch said again, commanding.

"I will gladly put this sword down," the cowboy replied, "in about ten seconds."

"NOW." Arch put a little extra mustard into his command. If the cowboy made so much as a move toward the fellow in the John Deere hat whose name Arch wasn't honestly sure he'd ever caught, he was going to be making a quick trip to Calhoun County Hospital, maybe take a flight from there to Chattanooga to have some bullets extracted.

"Okay," the cowboy said, voice laced with strain. "I'm going to start putting it down, very slowly. You know, just so you don't mistake my behavior for something … untoward." He started to slowly bend, lowering his sword and his body like he was very gradually moving toward a squat.

"You could speed it up a little," Arch said, annoyed. He'd been looking for action but would have preferred it stayed restricted to duty hours. Sheriff Reeve was going to be irritated if he had to pay overtime for this. Especially if it dragged on.

"No," the cowboy said, moving at the rate of about a half-inch per second, "I really can't."

Arch's gaze was drawn to the good ol' boy, the paper mill worker. His eyes were funny, lit up with a glow like someone was shining a light in them. Arch looked, just for a second, turning his head to see if there was something behind him, a light source or reflection that'd be causing it. "You okay?" Arch asked the fellow. He'd seen him before, knew the guy from when he'd worked security at one of the paper mill's company picnics down by the river, keeping the drinkers in line. They'd talked, a group of other guys and him, about college football, about UT's chances this year. They weren't great.

The man in the John Deere hat didn't respond, not in words. He let out a low growl, something that didn't even sound human, more like a dog crossed with a cat that'd caught its tail in a clamp, and he shook his head hard enough to break something. Nothing broke, though, not anything physical anyhow, but the man's face seemed to change, to loosen, like the flesh was sloshing around, draining toward his mouth the way the water went out of a toilet boil. What was replacing it was shadow, darkness, a bug's exoskeleton made out of shades of blackest night. Arch blinked once, then twice. He slapped a hand on his face, rubbed one eyelid, then the other, never closing them both. He had to be hallucinating. It wasn't any form of mind-altering substance, because Arch didn't truck with that stuff, but heck if what he was seeing wasn't something of that sort.

"You might want to step back," the cowboy said, and Arch wanted to say something to reply to him, but he couldn't find the words. The good ol' boy had turned into some shadowed thing, a monster with glowing red eyes, like they were the windows into the old furnace Arch's parents had in the house when he was a kid.

"What the—?" was all Arch had time to mutter before the thing in the John Deere hat came flying at the cowboy, fast as anything that ever crawled or skittered. The cowboy looked to be ready for it, though, and dodged back, taking a clumsy swipe with his sword as the John Deere hat went past. There was a squealing noise and something that sounded like clicking as the thing came back around for another pass, righting itself after missing the cowboy.

Arch considered shooting the cowboy, as he'd threatened, but frankly, the situation was all fouled up and that didn't seem the thing to do. Clearly something had happened to the good ol' boy. He was on PCP or something. There was really no other way to explain it.

The cowboy took another dodge back, almost whirling out of the way as the thing came at him again, and he tried to stop the good ol' boy with the sword—a pretty, one-handed thing—but he hit him with it and the good ol' boy kept coming, forcing him back further. There was enough of a gap between them that Arch could shoot without worrying about hitting something he wasn't supposed to, and he didn't even bother to call out. The good ol' boy in the John Deere hat had made his moves on the cowboy after a uniformed police officer was on the scene, and unless Arch missed his guess, pepper spray and a Taser weren't gonna do a damned thing to settle this down. The cowboy was actually defending himself against John Deere. And losing, even though he had a sword.

Arch fired the Glock three times. Double tapped John Deere in the head and put one in the body as an afterthought. The .40 bucked in his hands, the plastic pistol grip kicking with every pull of the trigger. The shots were good; Arch was proficient, having put in far more range time than was technically required with his weapon. He saw every one of the shots hit, but they didn't seem to do much of anything, barely staggering the thing in the John Deere hat. Instead of dropping like he should have, the thing seemed to almost shrug them off like they were nothing of serious concern, just walking right through them, heading for the cowboy.

The cowboy was ready this time, though, and before Arch got a chance to fire again the cowboy thrust out with the sword. Taking advantage of the moment's hesitation by the good ol' boy/thing, he thrust the blade where the throat should have been on the shadowed creature. Critter, Arch liked to think of it after seeing what it could do. A critter, a thing, like a mongrel dog that attacked anything that came at it. The cowboy hadn't even really come at it, but it damned sure wasn't a man. Not anymore, if it ever really had been.

There should have been a gurgling noise from where the cowboy had stabbed it, but there wasn't. It was more like a steady dripping, sped up, a tapping or clicking like something was slapping against something else. The darkness swirled around the thing, like a black hole had opened up and was devouring it. Crackles of orange like the outline of a flame ran through the dark that surrounded the thing, washing over it in slow motion. Tendrils of the dark flame consumed it one lick at a time until the feet disappeared last of all, dissolving to leave nothing on the sidewalk to show that the good ol' boy in the John Deere hat that Arch had met at a picnic once and talked UT football with had ever even existed.

"Well," the cowboy said, and let his sword clatter to the ground, "how was that for some action to break up the monotony of small-town life?"

Arch just stared at him for a few seconds then lowered the gun, letting it rest in a low safe position while he kept an eye on the cowboy's hands. "That … thing. He attacked you?"

"Was about to," the cowboy agreed, "when I drew my sword. Couldn't help himself, see. The Chu'ala, they have an aggressor response like no animal on earth. The minute he knew that I knew what he was, it was game on, and nothing was gonna stop it but the last buzzer. No time outs for them, they're straight-up killers."

Arch tried not to stare blankly, but then he cast another gaze at the spot where the good ol' boy had literally disappeared. That sort of thing just didn't happen, did it? "You called it a Chu'ala." Sounded like koala, but with a choo like choo-choo in front of it. "What is that?"

The cowboy stared back at him, half-smiling, hands on his knees like he was winded. "You probably don't wanna know, honestly. I mean, what you just saw? That sort of thing tends to be career-ending if you were to write a report about it, you know. They'll ship you off to the local Bellevue."

Arch hadn't even thought of that. "What was it?" Dogged, like he had to know. He did have to know, but he couldn't put a finger on why. This was the sort of crazed stuff he wouldn't have ever thought he'd encounter, and he'd had a teacher at the academy who was an Atlanta cop, told him stories about things he didn't think he'd ever see in Calhoun County. Definitely not something crazier than all that, even. A man turning into a devil-insect and then disappearing into shadows and night like he was being swallowed whole by it? That was far out of consideration.

"I told you," the cowboy said with an easy, not entirely sincere grin, "it was a Chu'ala."

"Like a chihuahua?" Arch raised a don't-give-me-no-bull cop face. He hadn't learned that at the academy. "Didn't look like no little yappy dog to me. It didn't even look human."

The cowboy gave a grudging nod of his head. "Well, you got that much, at least. Most people don't make that leap straightaway. You're right, it wasn't human." He gave a look left, then right, as though he half expected another of those things to come leaping out at him. "You mind if I pick up my sword?" Arch shook his head. "No?" The cowboy's disappointment seemed mild. "Well," there came a kind of exhausted, long sigh, "in that case … it's a demon. A Chu'ala is a demon of the old school, and when I stabbed it in the neck with my sword," he gestured at the blade that lay upon the grass, shining in the lamplight, "the rupture loosed his essence, sending him right back to whatever hell he came from." The cowboy said it all plain, matter-of-fact, like he was giving directions to Rogerson's just down the highway. He waited a second, watching Arch, watching the gears spin.

"A demon?" Arch's logical mind butted up against the problem once, then twice, then once again. He had no suspect, no body, no evidence of an assault, no victim—or attacker, as the case might have been—nothing but a cowboy with a sword, strolling through the town center of Midian just before midnight, getting into a fight with a man Arch thought he'd known, who had turned into something improbable, then promptly dissolved into shadow and disappeared, maybe back to hell, if indeed that's where he came from.

"Yeah," the cowboy agreed. "Sounds pretty fucked up, doesn't it? Like I said, you might wanna just stroll on away from this one and pretend you didn't see anything. It'd probably simplify your life." There was just a touch of apprehension under 'don't-give-a-damn' in the cowboy's tone. "I know it'd simplify mine if you did."

Arch pondered that for a moment as he slipped his Glock back in his holster. He was running it through his brain, trying to figure out how to explain it to the sheriff in a report—explain a man who didn't run away, didn't disappear by hiding behind something, but a guy who vanished, evaporated into the air itself. Trying to imagine explaining to Reeve that he'd been off duty and seen something staggering, absolutely amazing and impossible. Imagine having to file a report on it—which would technically mean he'd have to punch in, or be in violation of regulations. And that would go over … not so well.

He looked around the square. No lights were on, no sounds were made. His gunshots were loud, but not that uncommon in a rural area like Calhoun County. People shot in one of the fields behind the square from time to time, and firecrackers during July weren't exactly the most unusual of sounds. No cars, no lights, nothing. A quiet night in Midian. Not a soul about. He eyed the sword, and the cowboy took a step back from it. Arch took a couple steps forward, stooped and picked it up, looked at the fancy swirls of runes that made the blade look particularly intricate. "You think I should just let you go, I expect?"

"Well, of course," the cowboy said. "Doesn't everyone you catch hope that you'll just let them go?"

"Not all of them come at me with stories of demons and hell as alibis for what they've done, though. Almost none of them are strangers, in town for just an hour before they start waving a sword around and killing some poor bastard that works at the local paper mill by making them disappear like something out of a Criss Angel performance."

The cowboy inclined his head slightly. "I can see why this might be a little disturbing to you. It took me a little getting used to myself when my eyes first got opened to this sort of stuff. Might I suggest a little something to ease the passage …?"

The cowboy was ever so mild in his suggestion, and it made Arch just a little curious what he thought might make this easier in the slightest. This idea of demons and disappearing people that didn't really fit into Arch's world, not at all. "What's that?" Arch asked.

"We should go get a beer."

*

The cop hadn't let him have his sword back, but Hendricks wasn't all that worried about it, not yet. He'd gotten in the back of the patrol car, and the cop had put the sword up front with him after searching him for weapons. That had caused a tense moment, but he'd been up front with the officer. "I have a 1911 pistol in my belt," Hendricks had said. "My ID's in my back pocket, along with a permit to carry it."

The cop had taken the gun out of Hendricks's belt. The guy was big, broad, muscular, a black man who, if Hendricks had still been a gambler of any sort, he would have laid money on having been a football player at some point in his academic career. He didn't just have the build for it; he had the power. The cop was at least six foot two, and even with his Marine training, Hendricks wouldn't have wanted to get in a scrape with the fellow. No chance. Demons were easier, because you could just kill them. Fighting humans sucked.

After the cop had taken Hendricks's gun and sword, and asked him to remove his coat, Hendricks got in the back of the cop car, a new model Ford Explorer that rode real nice. He was tempted to ask which he was headed for, a bar or jail, but they buzzed right on past the sheriff's office without turning, though Hendricks caught a backwards look in the rear-view at him as they neared, as though the cop expected him to crack or something at the prospect of going to jail. It wouldn't exactly be the highlight of Hendricks's night, that was for sure, but a jail cell still beat the hell out of being devoured, guts-first, by a raging Chu'ala in the town square.

Besides, he at least got to keep his cowboy hat. That was something.

There was a glaring patch of neon up ahead, and Hendricks recognized the same stretch of strip malls he'd seen when he'd come into town from the interstate. The Wal-Mart was up there and a few other stores, a fireworks outlet, and a bar with a red neon sign blaring the name "Fast Freddie's." It sounded like a pretty jerkoff place, but Hendricks wasn't too picky, being both hungry and parched and not having had anything to eat nor drink nor even had a chance to piss since being picked up at the Cracker Barrel outside Nashville hours earlier by the trucker. The last concern was still mild; the first two were growing in importance rapidly. He was parched and hungry enough to skin a coyote and eat it ass-first.

Fast Freddie's was a shitty looking place, all wooden eaves and paneling outside, like it was supposed to be an authentic Texas roadhouse. Old Father Time had clearly had his way with the joint, though, and it was faded enough that even the red neon sign looked worn. Hendricks would have bet that it looked like hell during the daytime, probably like it had been damned near forgotten by the owners, needing all manner of improvements. Still, Midian was a one-horse town, or possibly less, maybe a one-mule town, or even lower, a one-cat town or something. It was damned small; a micropolis, he'd heard this type of place called before. It only looked as big as it did because it served the rest of Calhoun County, drawing in people from the rural reaches of the county to the surprisingly wide array of commerce it offered.

When they were in the parking lot, the big cop turned over his shoulder and looked back at him. "Your weapons stay in the car. I'll listen to your story over one beer. If I don't like the sound of it, your next ride is to the sheriff's station."

"Can I get a last meal, too?" Hendricks grinned.

The deputy was impassive. "If you want. Not sure I'd trust Fast Freddie's to handle my dietary needs, but it's your digestive tract."

Hendricks let the grin hang. "You paying?"

"Nope," the cop said and stepped out, shoes squeaking on the wet asphalt.

Hendricks shrugged. It wasn't like he didn't have money. He waited for the cop to open the door and considered himself lucky he wasn't cuffed. When it opened, he stepped out, walking slowly in front of the deputy, leading the way without much concern. It was understandable, after all; the deputy wanted to keep an eye on his potential prisoner.

Stepping inside Fast Freddie's was like taking the dial of the time machine and spinning it back to the Old West, if the Old West had had neon signs. After thinking about it for a moment, Hendricks decided maybe it was more like a rodeo king's worst nightmare, the inside of this place, some garish cross between a honky-tonk and a bullrider's bar, or maybe more of a caricature of what some jackass thought those things oughta look like rather than what they really did. It didn't matter either way, though, because the people at the bar were there for one reason alone—to drink—and they were all about that serious business when Hendricks walked in with the deputy just behind him. He imagined the cop's khakis probably turned a few eyes his way, then realized that in this sort of bar, all the eyes were on a pullstring attached to the door handle anyway, and whenever someone walked in they got the once over from the entire patronage. In most cases, this was not a good thing. In one instance, though …

A damned fine-looking girl wearing a V-necked white t-shirt came flouncing up, on her seventh or eight drink if Hendricks were gambling (and in this case he would have, gladly), jeans too tight by half for anywhere but a bar or a rodeo, but there were no complaints from him on that score, not for this girl. She was blond, and not just perky but pretty, wasted on this establishment. He tried to draw himself up a little straighter, and for a half a flash he let himself imagine that she might actually be coming to the door to talk to him.

That image was dispelled a half second later when she went straight up to the cop. "You came!" she said and gave the guy a big hug. Here the height difference was blatantly obvious; the deputy was a damned giant, and this girl was average height. Hendricks had never really been insecure about his height, but then he was a shade under six feet and always considered that reasonable. He'd been in the same barracks with a guy in boot camp on Parris Island who was even taller than the deputy at his side and always felt bad for the fella because what they'd always said about tall guys being well-hung had turned out not to be true for this guy. To the disappointment of a girl in his training platoon. Of course she told everyone. Poor bastard.

"I'm uh …" The deputy looked just a little discomfited to Hendricks's eyes. More than a little, actually, the man looked like he'd been dunked in cold water and forced to confess to a particularly heinous crime, all in one expression. "I'm just here for a drink with my friend …" The deputy looked at him, gave him a pointed, *Help me out, pal* kind of look.

"Lafayette Hendricks, ma'am," he said doffing his cowboy hat to the blond lady. She looked a little younger than him, not much, probably twenty-two, twenty-three. Her blue eyes glimmered with vague interest, he thought, but he hadn't seen that in a long time and wasn't practiced enough to tell whether she was just being polite or if it was something more.

"This is Erin Harris," the deputy said, nodding to the blond. "She's the dispatcher down at the station."

"Name like Lafayette, you ain't gonna start speaking French to me?" she asked. Maybe that was interest.

"Not likely," Hendricks said, keeping it cool. "I'm from Wisconsin. Can't speak a lick of French 'cept for maybe *merci* and *oui*."

"I think, technically," Erin said, beset by a case of the giggles that was probably induced by the bourbon that he could smell on her breath, "that the *oui* would come before the *merci*." Another giggle, and it was cute. "But I might be out of practice."

Hendricks wondered if he was blushing visibly. There was every chance she was going to regret this flirtation later, if she even remembered it. "I'm afraid I'll have to trust your experience with the language is greater than my own, because mine is pretty limited."

She giggled again then stopped as the cop cleared his throat. "Sorry, Erin," the cop said, "I'm just here to have a beer with my friend."

She blinked, kind of wide-eyed, and Hendricks was sure it made her even cuter. "You're gonna have a beer? Like an actual one? Holy shit." She shook her head, and it looked like she almost lost her balance. "Well, okay, then," she touched the deputy all around his collar, then tried to straighten it but left it popped out on one side. "Sorry."

"It's okay, I got it." The deputy's mild chagrin was obvious as he fiddled with his collar, straightening it out.

"I'll just leave you boys alone, then," she said, and Hendricks caught the first hint of slurring in her speech. "But when you get done, you should come over and join me and the boys for another round. I would definitely buy you a beer, Officer Stan." She shuffled away under her own power, barely, not quite falling down drunk but definitely happier than she would have been without the alcohol coursing through her veins.

When she was gone, the cop she'd called Officer Stan guided Hendricks over to a corner table and gestured at the barman by holding up two fingers and getting a nod in return. "I thought you didn't drink?" Hendricks asked.

"I haven't had a beer in two years," the deputy returned.

"But you have good enough code with the bartender that you can hold up two fingers and he knows what to bring you?"

The deputy shrugged. "All beer tastes the same to me—bad. Reckon he'll bring me whatever he sells the most of."

"We could shoot whiskey if you'd prefer," Hendricks suggested. He'd gladly shoot whiskey, and lots of it. Mainly because he was likely to be hurting tomorrow anyway, courtesy of the Chu'ala. Why not add a little distraction behind the eyes, just to give the bruises a competition for what would hurt the most in the morning?

"No, thanks," the deputy said.

"So the pretty blond you work with called you Officer Stan," Hendricks said as he took in the place again. The girl who'd talked to the deputy was in the corner with a couple of other guys and looking over at him. Maybe some interest. Maybe. "You got a first name, or is it Stan and she's just real formal?"

"Everyone calls me Arch," came the reply. Damn, the guy was tall, like a mountain sitting across the table from him, and forbidding, too, near humorless.

"Why's that?"

"Because my momma named me Archibald, and it's a silly name that I don't care for."

Hendricks watched him, gave him a little smile. "That's all right, no one calls me Lafayette, either."

"Yeah, I heard you call yourself—what? Lafayette—"

"Lafayette Jackson Hendricks is what my momma called me," he said, "when she was mad at me about something—which was a fair amount. But no one's called me Lafayette since my momma died, and no one calls me Jack on account of I make it clear to them that I won't abide it, so I pretty much go by Hendricks. Once upon a time it was Staff Sergeant Hendricks but now it's plain old Hendricks." Hendricks started to go on but one of the waitresses dropped a couple of bottles of Budweiser off at the table. He blanched as he took his first sip and saw the same from the deputy. "Bud's not to my liking, either."

"Oh, yeah?" The deputy eyed him carefully. "You tell much difference between the different kinds of beer?"

"Not the national brands," Hendricks said. "Back home in Western Wisconsin, where I come from, they got a brew called Leinenkugels that beats the shit outta anything you find elsewhere. I went all over in the Marines. The only other things I found I really liked were some Greek beer I can't even remember the name of and Guinness."

Arch paused, surveying Hendricks real quietly. "This discussion of microbrews is real classy, but let's cut right through the bunk. What happened back there?"

Hendricks grinned again. It was getting to be natural for him this evening, and it hadn't been like that for him in years. "Like I said, you sure you want to delve very deep in that? It's a long way down that rabbit hole, Alice. You might be sorry you ever opened your eyes to that world because it's damned hard to climb back up after you take that trip, and things don't tend to be the same after you take the first step."

Not even a moment's hesitation. "Yes, I want to know what happened out there. You said demon. Demon, like from hell?"

"Dunno if he's from hell," Hendricks said, taking another swill—literally, and not liking it much. "But I know he's a demon, like the creatures of old. They look like humans, 'til you know what to look for.

Different breeds, too, species, like animals, but they blend in with humans most of the time. At least, most do."

Arch was listening, taking it all in. "All right, so if they're demons, what are they here for?"

Hendricks gave the barest shrug. "If you're talking about in the larger sense of it, in the 'Why are we all here? What is our greater purpose?' sense, then fuck if I know. If you mean, why are they here in this town, right now, that I might have an answer for, though I'm not sure you're gonna like it."

"Lay it on me." It was hard to tell whether this deputy, Arch, was humoring him or seriously listening, but either way, he was paying attention, so Hendricks went on.

"The way it was explained to me, there are certain places on the earth that flare at any given moment, become 'hotspots' if you will, that pull in demons like the light on a bugzapper—but without the zapper, I suppose. They're drawn to them, these bursts of … I dunno, mystical or whatever activity, and they come congregating into whatever town or place is throwing off that vibe. Right now, it's here in Calhoun County."

"Uh huh," Arch's arms were folded now, which was new. Hendricks didn't like the look of that. "How do you know about this mystical stuff?"

Hendricks shrugged. "Someone told me about it, and I was just about as disbelieving as you are. Course, that was about five years and eighteen hotspots ago, so I've since developed a little faith that my mentor wasn't just blowing smoke up my ass, but when I was sitting in your chair it was all, 'Yeah, right,' and 'Whatever.' Probably about what you're thinking now. I was also thinking, 'Bullshit,' but you don't strike me as much of the swearing type, so maybe you have a clean way to say it."

"Malarkey."

Hendricks raised an eyebrow in surprise. "Really? You're gonna go with that, huh?"

"It's gotten me this far."

"'Bullshit' sounds more—"

"Profane?"

"That, too," Hendricks agreed. "But I would have said serious."

Arch rolled his eyes, which Hendricks got the suspicion wasn't very characteristic of the man, either. But half his beer was gone, obvious by the light shining through the brown bottle. "You gotta swear like a sailor to be serious, huh?"

"I don't do anything like a sailor," Hendricks said with a frown. "I was a Marine."

"Whatever. You know what I meant." Arch took a swig and frowned, but it was a long pull and it looked like he'd just about finished the bottle. "I'm almost done with my beer and I'm still not really believing you."

"Fair enough," Hendricks said. "You did just see a man turn into something decidedly un-human, then disappear after being stabbed in the neck, though. What would be your logical, non-demon explanation for that? You know, if you had to explain it. Extra points if you manage to steer clear of any accusations involving me doping you with hallucinogens, because I plainly didn't."

Arch cocked an eyebrow at him. "Some guy I barely know just got—I don't know, devoured by shadows while I watched—I'm not ruling out hallucinogens. For all I know you sprayed some kind of gas in the air and I'm tripping right now." He held up the bottle. "Which would explain why I'm having a beer with you rather than dragging you to jail. Might be the only thing that makes sense in this case, actually."

"He didn't disappear," Hendricks explained, keeping his cool though he felt his mouth go dry. He really, really didn't want to spend a night in jail. Or two. Or three. Anything more than possession of the sword would be hard to prove, but the sword was pretty rare and he didn't want to risk losing it. Or have shit go down out in the outside world while he was sweating away in county jail. "Most demons don't have bodies like us, exactly. What they have is like a shell, a kind of a veneer of human flesh on the outside that hides their true appearance. When I stabbed him in the neck, I was breaking the shell, which caused his essence to be drawn back to wherever the hell it came from. Kind of breaks their hold on this … dimension? Realm? Whatever, I've never really understood the explanation I've gotten on that one."

The bar was smoky, but Arch's gaze was smokier. "You went after this thing to kill it, but you don't really understand what happened to it?"

"Actually, I went up to the guy to ask for directions to the cheapest motel in town, but I recognized him, he knew I recognized him, and he knew I knew, which caused him to have to throw down, because that's how

Chu'ala demons act when they feel threatened in the slightest. I would have been perfectly happy just to get my directions and be on about my evening, but once that happened, we kind of got locked on course."

"Still doesn't explain why you're carrying a sword to fight these things when you don't really know what they're all about."

"I know enough," Hendricks said, keeping his irritation under wraps. "The full explanation is somewhere between a genius-level physics problem and something involving mystical elements that are way more spiritual than I give a fuck about. I know the mechanics, I know how to kill them, and so I stick to what I know. And I carry the sword because the sword kills them."

"How?" Arch asked.

"Mystical stuff," Hendricks said. "Breaks through—"

"Yeah, yeah," Arch waved him off.

"So," Hendricks went on after a pause in which Arch stared at his beer for what felt like several minutes, "you still haven't answered me about what you think it was you saw tonight."

"See, I don't have to explain it to you," Arch said, and it was damned obvious he was cross as hell. "I have to explain it to the sheriff, my boss, about how I think I witnessed a murder, except I don't have a victim, I don't have a body, I don't have anything except some cowboy with a sword and a pistol."

"Hey, the pistol's legal," Hendricks said. "My carry permit is valid for Tennessee."

"The sword ain't, though."

Hendricks gave a weak shrug. "You'd let me carry a gun but not a sword? So you charge me with … uh …"

"Let's not go there," Arch said darkly. "I could charge you with any number of things. That's not at issue, me finding nominal violations of the law. My issue is whether I want to believe some jackwagon who steps into town and his first night starts stirring up some deeply dark mystical juju of a kind I don't even know I believe in. If I let you walk, is this gonna become a pattern? You gonna go out and raise some more havoc, kill some more of those things?"

"I try to keep it out of the public eye, but yeah," Hendricks replied, and finished his beer with a long pull. "Trust me when I tell you that these demons are not the sort of thing you want walking around your town, in human skin or without. They're killers, murderers, and cause all manner of mischief that goes unreported. Mysterious disappearances follow in their wake like fleas trail a dirty old hound dog. Things burn when they're around, mental illness leaps right up through the roof. Murder rates skyrocket. "

Hendricks leaned across the table. "Things don't turn out so well for these hotspots. Look at Detroit, look at New Orleans. Both of them have had flare-ups at various points in the last fifty years—hell, Detroit's been a hotspot some twenty five times, some worse than others. Small towns, though, they get real bad. Turn to ghost towns in some cases." He lowered his voice. "There was a town in Alaska last year, just dropped off the map, five hundred people gone by the time it was done flaring. You don't want this thing going unchallenged, not here, not anywhere."

Arch stared back at him. "There gonna be more like you coming?"

Hendricks took a long, slow breath, let the tobacco smoke in the air waft in. He didn't smoke, but when he was drinking it didn't bother him like it did when he was sober. He almost kind of liked it. "Probably, but not for a while. There's kind of a lot going on for my kind right now."

"Oh, yeah?" Arch asked. "You a … what? A demon hunter or something?"

"Something like that," Hendricks said. "And there are definitely demon hunters, and some of them might even come this way, though I'd suspect it will be a long while before they do."

"Why's that?"

Hendricks took another breath of the secondhand smoke, and could almost feel it calm his nerves. "Because this is the eighteenth hot spot in the world that's flaring right now." He wanted a cigarette and he didn't even smoke. It had been a long day.

"You say that like it should mean something to me."

"Sorry," Hendricks said with some genuine contrition. "Didn't mean to be so damned vague. So, this is number eighteen. That's kind of unusual. There are usually less."

"Less?" Arch's hands were back behind his head now, and he waved off the waitress when she came by to make another pass to see if they wanted another round. "Like, ten?" Hendricks shook his head. "Five? Four?" He kept shaking his head, and used his index finger to point down, tapping at the table the entire time.

"More like one," Hendricks said, gingerly, and he shook the empty beer bottle, wishing it was full again. He looked up at the deputy with all seriousness, though. "Usually, there's only ever one at a time. So, as you might guess with eighteen going at once … we're in some new territory, here."

*

Hollywood didn't want to stay at the dairy farm, not with the smell. He hated it, and it was in his suit, his fucking ten-thousand-dollar suit that he'd gotten on Savile Row in London. He knew it was in his ponytail, too, and he was going to have to exfoliate like crazy to get the smell of it off his skin. He had Sleeveless driving his car for him, chauffeuring, and had made sure they'd gotten towels from the farmer's house for Sleeveless to sit on. No point in soiling the town car any more than was necessary, after all.

They were heading toward the interstate, maybe even as far back as Chattanooga, because he doubted there was much more than a fleabag motel in this town, and frankly, there was a lot to be said for being able to get a meal with some decent organic produce. You didn't know what you were getting, after all. If his body was going to be the temple of Ygrusibas, it made sense to feed it things that would make it better, not worse. Also, none of the local motels had a gym. Or Wifi. Fucking hicks, fucking sticks.

"Something going on up here," Sleeveless said as they drew close to the interstate. It was an hour or so to Chattanooga, and there had to be at least somewhere he could stay there, somewhere that would take his Black Card and give him some semblance of order, something approaching—maybe like a lesser version, like tier one instead of tier five—the treatment he got in L.A. They knew how to do shit right. They should, after all. The whole place was built by and for demons.

Sleeveless slowed the car as they drove past the parking lot of a neon-lit hellhole that a sign proclaimed to be Fast Freddie's. Hollywood looked out the window, staring into the dark night as they went on, taking in the scene in the parking lot. It was almost nothing, really, something so subtle that only their kind would notice.

There were two men standing next to a cop car. It wasn't so much what they were wearing in terms of clothes—though one of them wore a cowboy hat, like he was what? John Travolta or something? No, it was what they were wearing over the clothes that caught the eye. It dusted them and clung to them like skin, so obvious that it practically glowed to those who knew what to look for.

"Looks like those boys just killed them a demon," Sleeveless said from the driver's seat.

Hollywood couldn't find it in him to disagree. It was obvious; they were just doused in the essence. "One of the locals?"

"Could be." Sleeveless slowed the car further, and rolled down the window. "There were a decent number of us around before things started heating up, and lots of strangers been coming into town lately with the rising." The smell of sulfur was obvious even at this distance, and Hollywood wanted to gag even more now, needed to get to something approaching a five-star hotel, preferably one with multiple shower heads. "Should we stop, maybe put 'em down?"

Hollywood shook his head. "No. Not right now. Probably just some brain-dead, thrill-killer demon hunter in town because of the flare. Doesn't mean anything to us, necessarily." He brought one of his well-manicured hands up to his mouth, pondered chewing the nail. It was a nasty habit he had, something his manicurist hated but was paid good money to repair. Too bad she was in L.A. "Have one of the boys keep an eye on them, though, maybe watch them in town, see what they're up to. Find out where they stay." He motioned for Sleeveless to roll up the window, which he did, and the car accelerated toward the on ramp, taking the turn and heading south toward Chattanooga. "If it turns out they're going to be a problem, well, hey … I could use some more warm bodies, at least until I figure out this ritual. After that … they won't so much be a problem for any of us."

Chapter 3

"I'm going to let you go—for now," Arch announced as they walked out the door of Fast Freddie's, Arch wondering how much beer he'd had. He decided he'd breathalyze himself just to be safe before he started his car. He'd waited an hour after finishing his beer, just chatting idly with Hendricks. The fact that the cowboy was ex-military weighed in his favor. They'd talked about the war, how Hendricks had been in Iraq, and somewhere between that and the crazy talk about demons rising, Arch had figured on letting the man go. None of it made any rational sense, but then again a great many things Arch believed in required some level of faith. And Arch was definitely a man of faith. The stuff Hendricks was talking about was straight out of the Bible, things the preacher even usually shied away from talking about at the pulpit on Sundays. Arch wasn't sure he believed it was happening, not now, but explaining it to Sheriff Reeve would be a trip in and of itself. Assuming it was even possible.

"For now?" Hendricks didn't grin, not this time. "Well, I appreciate that."

"You're not leaving town anytime soon, are you?" Arch asked him. Hendricks just shook his head, big cowboy hat brim waving left and right. "Good. Where you gonna be staying?"

"Cheap hotel?" Hendricks asked him.

"The Sinbad, down by the off ramp over there," Arch said and pointed his finger. He caught a glimpse of a sedan slowing down as it passed by on the old highway. He gave it a glance but not much more. He was standing by his Explorer, after all, and people tended to slow down at the sight of a cop car. Probably wise. Most cops might not have leapt up into the car to pursue and give them a speeding ticket, but Arch wasn't most cops. "Cheapest place around. It'll run you about twenty-five a night. A word of caution, though—"

"Let me guess," Hendricks said. "It's not fancy."

"That might be understating it just a tad."

"I don't need much," Hendricks said. "A bed, running water."

"It'll have one of those," Arch said. "Probably."

There was a brief awkward silence, then Hendricks spoke again. "Can I have my stuff back?"

"Right," Arch said and reached into the passenger side of his car. He tossed the big black drover coat to Hendricks. Once he had it on, Arch handed him the .45. Hendricks waited expectantly, a little anxious. Arch hesitated as he picked up the sword and looked at it. It wasn't terribly long, probably a two-and-a-half-foot blade, but razor sharp, only an inch wide. It could put a hurting on a person, but obviously not as bad as the pistol, which there was no doubt Hendricks was cleared to carry. Arch had seen the Wisconsin permit, and it was current. Arch ran a finger along the side of the blade, taking care to stay away from the edge. It almost looked silver in the light, but he would have guessed stainless steel and wicked sharp. It was an elegant thing, with twists and runes added, probably to make it look extra cool. "If this ends up in somebody's belly, I will track you to the end of the earth and make you pay for my mistake."

"The end of the county, you mean?" Hendricks said without a smile. Arch was expecting one, like being flippant was just second nature to the ex-Marine. "Don't worry, I don't use it on people, just demons, which means, by definition, you'll never see a corpse with a stab wound from it."

That didn't make Arch feel much better. He didn't cringe but definitely winced on the inside. Demons were a hard thing to swallow, harder than the idea of a murder taking place in Calhoun County. Those did happen, every once in a while. Demons were a little too far off the wall. "Just keep out of trouble, okay?"

Hendricks gave him a look like, *Yeah, right*, and Arch didn't even bother to argue. "Thanks for the understanding," Hendricks said finally.

"I don't think I do understand," Arch said and got in his car, slamming the door behind him. He watched the cowboy walk off back toward the hotel, wondering if he'd come even close to doing the right thing here.

*

Hendricks was walking along in the hot Tennessee night, betting the temperature was still somewhere north of eighty, even after midnight, listening to the slap of his cowboy boots crunching against the gravel on the shoulder of the road and keeping his eyes fixed on the sign for the Sinbad motel. "Heh," he said. Sinbad wasn't a terrible name for an off-ramp motel like this. Back home they used to derisively call the local one the "Fuck-and-Run." It was a fairly accurate representation of what happened there. Hendricks decided he liked the Sinbad better. It winked at the purpose of the place, removed the need for a nickname like the "Fuck-and-run." Probably didn't stop it, though.

He hadn't stopped drinking when Arch had, preferring instead to have a few more. It seemed like a good idea at the time, but it had made him want to hang around the bar a little longer when the cop wanted to leave. Since he'd been in the custody of Arch at the time, technically, that wasn't sound thinking. So even though he'd have preferred to stick around, maybe keep an eye on that blond, Erin, see what she was up to, he didn't. He went with Arch to hear the verdict. After that, he'd realized he was too tired to keep going.

On reflection, getting drunk in front of a deputy sheriff who's trying to decide whether or not to release you maybe wasn't the sharpest thinking. On the other hand, going to jail sober didn't sound like much fun either.

He was on the overpass when he realized he was being followed, the sound of footsteps behind him in the quiet night being occasionally drowned out by the nighttime semis and cars passing underneath the bridge on the interstate below. He cast a quick look back and saw a silhouette, a small one. He knew immediately that it wasn't Arch, this silhouette being practically half his size, or more like three-quarters and thin. Petite. Like a woman.

He took a quick breath and hoped for the best, that it was Erin following him. He wouldn't complain. It had been a damned long time, almost a half-decade, since he'd felt a woman's touch. The alcohol and the fact that he'd already had one human conversation today was loosening him up, making it worse, if that were possible. He was too used to being isolated, which made it easier.

"Hey," he said to the figure he thought was Erin. She got a little closer and a passing car's headlights illuminated her as she stopped about ten feet from him, just a little ways back. It wasn't Erin. Damned sure not.

In the light of the headlights he saw red hair, deep red, and cold, pale skin with fierce eyes that he couldn't tell the color of in the dark. She was cute, damned cute, but looked a little hawkish, and she had a bit of a standoffish attitude as she halted about ten feet away from him. The truck blew past them and he was left looking at her silhouette again, just the side of her face visible in the light of the neon sign from the motel behind him. His hand went for the hilt of his sword automatically, but she spoke before it got there.

"You won't need that."

"I won't?" Hendricks didn't relax at all; he kept his hand right where it was. "Why not?"

She studied him like he was nothing more than a specimen, something peculiar and barely worthy of note—no emotion, no interest, but like a predator keeping a wary eye on prey that was about to run off. "Like you, I am not looking for a fight."

"Well, if you're like me," Hendricks said, keeping his hand right where it was at, "then you don't always get what you're looking for, especially as it relates to fighting."

"That probably says more about you than it does about your opponents," the woman said.

"What's your name?" Hendricks asked, still wary.

She hesitated. "I've been called many things but most recently Starling."

"Starling? Like the bird?"

She cocked her head, her red hair even more aglow in the neon light. "Close enough."

"Why are you following me, Starling?" Hendricks asked. "I mean, normally I wouldn't mind if a pretty girl followed me back to my hotel, but it feels a little strange when she's doing it while walking behind me instead of at my side, you know?"

"No," Starling replied. "I don't know." She paused. "I followed you to tell you that the reason you think you are here is not the reason you are here."

Hendricks watched her, trying to decide exactly how drunk he was. "So … you're saying I'm not here for the hotspot? Did I catch your drift correctly?"

She stared back at him. Her eyes didn't glow in the dark, they were just pools of black and shadow that didn't seem to catch even a little of the neon light. "You caught it. There's more going on in this town than just a hotspot burning off negative emanations."

He held back on shaking his head, knowing that such a simple action didn't have a hope of clearing it and would likely make it worse. "So … what, then?"

She peered at him. "Far more than you've been warned of. Far more than even *she* knows … yet."

Hendricks didn't even pause, felt the rush of drunkenness in his head. "You sure about that? *She* knows an awful lot."

The redhead shook hers. "She doesn't know about this. Not yet. No one does."

"What exactly is it that she doesn't know?" If things got any more confusing, Hendricks was going to need a translator to get out of the drunken fuzz. Or at least a tape recorder to play it back later when he could understand it.

"Who's at work here," Starling said. "What they're doing. Why they're here. Where they'll go next, after it's done. And … why this is the most important hotspot of all the ones currently flaring."

Hendricks stared at her. She was pretty gorgeous, he was sure of that, even if he was more than a little impaired. Kind of had a cool detachment, though, no warmth like that Erin had had. "I can't decide if you're being really damned cryptic or I'm just drunk."

Starling stared back at him without answering. Before he could say anything else, she walked casually to her right, took a high step over the concrete rail and jumped off the side of the overpass. He wanted to react, to say something, to smart off and ask her if it was something he'd said, but he didn't, he just bolted for the side of the bridge to gawk over, see her crash down. It was a long drop to the freeway below. The problem was, when he looked down, it was all black pavement and grass to the sides; even the white divider lines between lanes were completely invisible. All that was down there was darkness.

"Well, hell," Hendricks said, his voice echoing across the quiet lanes of the interstate, "that was an awfully dramatic exit."

*

The moment Arch's key hit the lock she was on him, a blur of motion that hit him in the chest with a quiet thump and a half-screamed, "I was worried! You weren't answering your phone." The accusation hung heavy on all of it, every word, and he felt himself cringe deep. "It's so unlike you."

He gently disentangled himself from his wife as he shut the door. "I'm fine. Just had a work issue that needed to be resolved, and it took me a little while to resolve it."

She wrinkled her nose. "Reeve gave you overtime?"

"Ah, no," Arch said, clicking the heavy deadbolt in place. "It was something that had to get handled off the clock."

"Oh." Her hair was blond right now, but she changed it with the seasons. She tended to go red or auburn with it in the fall, and even tried raven once in winter. Alison Longholt Stan was a pretty fashionable lady, he reflected, and had been for as long as he'd known her. Even being the assistant manager of one of her father's grocery store looked good on her. She'd convinced her daddy to change the color of the polo shirts that the managers wore to best suit her complexion. Arch had no doubt if she had some dramatic shift in pigment in the future, from an overdone fake tan, maybe, she could convince him to change the colors temporarily to whatever best fit her. Not that it mattered, it wasn't as though she would get fired for showing up in a different-colored shirt. "You know you were supposed to be home a couple hours ago."

"I know," Arch said, easing his keys onto the table by the door, listening to them clatter on the glass. The apartment smelled like supper, like she'd cooked something good, something hearty. There was a lot of fresh produce showing up from the local farms now, things that could just about make a meal of themselves. They'd eaten like that some nights during the summer, no meat, just vegetables. It wasn't Arch's favorite way to do things, but it was okay when it was all fresh like that. "I'm sorry."

"It's all right," she said, hugging him again, her head pressed against his uniform, face pushing into his chest. It took him a minute to realize she was sniffing him. "Why do you smell like smoke? And beer." She came off him in rough amazement, confusion clouding her pretty face. "You don't even drink."

"I had one beer," he admitted, "like I said, I needed to work something out."

"Uh huh," she said, just absolutely flummoxed. It wasn't like he'd ever done this before, or given her reason for suspicion. "You weren't working it out with Erin Harris, were you?"

"I saw her there, at Fast Freddie's," Arch said, "but I wasn't there with her, no."

"Okay," she said, but there was still a little concern there. He knew it wasn't something she was going to press; the advantage of small-town living was that tomorrow she'd be sure to hear from someone who'd been in Fast Freddie's that he was there with Hendricks, not a woman. She brightened just a little. "I hope you have some energy left."

"A little," he said, hesitant.

"Oh, come on, Arch," she said, a little plaintive. "I'm on day one of ovulating, and if we want to have a baby, I need you to—"

"I know, I know," he said, feeling his own discomfort magnify as she rubbed a hand along his chest. "Let me shower first? Been a long day."

"Okay," she said and gave him a full kiss. She hesitated and made a face as he started down the short hallway to the bathroom. "Maybe brush your teeth, too?"

*

Hendricks flicked the switch as he dragged into the motel room. It was everything that had been promised for twenty bucks a night. He'd negotiated a better rate for a week's stay. The odds weren't good that the hotspot would dry up in less than seven day's, and cash was the king of all fungible assets. He'd paid upfront and the terms had gotten suddenly more generous.

The room was all done in one shade, something between mauve and taupe, a tragic blend that probably should have died aborning. Instead it lingered here, in a motel on the far edge of nowhere, in a room with a lonely double bed with a threadbare comforter that was just a little too crimson for the rest of the room. Hendricks didn't know interior design, but he recognized what didn't work, and this sure as shit didn't.

The place had a smell like it'd been used for fucking and running a few too many times; a sweaty stink of bodies that had accumulated over years and years that no air freshener could touch. Like a locker room that had been given a cursory cleaning. He fiddled with the air conditioner, a monstrosity stretched out under the window. With a click, it turned on, filling the humid, warm and stuffy room with the sounds of air blowing and machinery humming beneath it. A faintly cool breeze blew out of the vent on top.

Hendricks peeled off his coat and threw it onto the chair in the corner, a sad, faded recliner that was right at home with the rest of the decor. He set the hat upside down upon the dresser delicately and looked at himself in the mirror above the sink, which was conveniently out in the main area of the room. His dark hair was sweated down into place, molded by the hat. He'd seen the guys who pull off a hat in the movies, and their hair was all sculpted perfection underneath. His looked like hell. He didn't even bother to fix it. What was the point, after all?

He peeled off his black t-shirt, which was stuck to his body after a long day's ride and then the fight and subsequent time in the bar followed by the walk to the motel. The steady combo of going from hot outside to cold indoors with air conditioning had affixed it to his skin, and it made a noise as he removed it. He was in pretty good shape, the product of a workout routine and calisthenics he undertook every morning. It gave him abs, gave him pecs, some pretty nice ones, too. Not that anyone would notice under the drover coat. That was okay, though, or it had been for the last few years. There was a bruise under his arm from the fight with the Chu'ala. He stared at himself in the mirror before kicking off his cowboy boots.

He wasn't sure how much longer he could keep this up. In Tulsa he'd scraped with a really nasty beast that had broken his arm. That'd been weeks of recovery, but he'd been fortunate enough to kill the thing before it had finished him off. It was a close one, though, the most recent of more injuries than he wanted to count. Too many.

Luck was a fickle thing for guys in his profession, and the girls too, few of them as there were. Time was, you'd run across the same people in new hotspots, and most of the time you'd meet with a grudging respect, a professional nod. Same faces, new places. Even before the sudden proliferation of hotspots, the faces he had remembered from the hotspots he'd "grown up" in when he started out had begun to disappear. Every once in a while he'd have beers with some of the other old pros, and they'd talk about how so-and-so had hung it up, retired, but more often how such-and-such had been found dead, killed by a demon if it wasn't one of the ones that ate you afterward. And there were plenty that just disappeared. They'd tip another back in honor, and that was probably all the acknowledgment that poor bastard ever got. Lonely business, killing demons.

He put his fingers on the bruise and felt himself blanch. It wasn't too bad, but it wasn't done forming yet. It wasn't always like this, but it had been this way long enough that he was just about used to being bruised all the time. Fuck. He hadn't even been looking for a fight. He cursed the Chu'ala. What a bastard, throwing down like that. Having to spill everything to the deputy was worse, though. It wasn't like it was the first time Hendricks had gotten into a public scrape, but it was the first time he'd ever been confronted about it afterward. By a cop, no less. Most people just thought he was fighting, and tended to skitter off when he pulled the sword. He only pulled the gun when he got truly desperate—and once when a Tuskun demon he'd been after had turned out to have a human sidekick, a partner in crime. That wasn't much fun.

He blinked at himself in the mirror, his brown eyes looking more than a little bleary. He felt old at twenty-five. He shouldn't, but it had been a long five years. It felt longer than the two he'd been in the Corps, even with the time he'd spent in Iraq, which was saying something, because that hadn't been much of a picnic.

In all the time he'd been killing demons, he'd never—not once—spilled it all to anyone like he had with Arch at the bar. It couldn't even be blamed on drink, because he'd gotten drunk with truckers, with strangers, even a few rodeo cowboys one night after a brutal fight outside Cheyenne. He'd looked worse than the guy that had just gotten ejected off a bull to land on his neck. Took some doing. He'd never spilled to any of them, not even after a ton of beers. But a Tennessee sheriff's deputy pointed a gun at him—like that hadn't ever happened before—and he'd folded without even a single drink and just laid it all out. Fuck.

"Must be getting old," he told the face in the mirror. And lonely. He didn't say that part out loud, though.

*

Arch usually slept well after being with his wife—in his less guarded moments he would call it making love, but never anything cruder than that—but last night he hadn't slept well at all. He had the early shift, daytime, and had just fallen asleep at some point after five when the alarm went off at six. He fended off Alison's gentle suggestions for a repeat of last night's activities. Not that he might not have been convinced with a little effort on her part, but he knew that she'd be after him for it again that evening, so he took a pass. Normally, he would have gladly gone for it again. This morning, however, he was distracted.

He rubbed his eyes as he guided the Ford Explorer into the parking space in front of the sheriff's station, shifting it into park and removing the keys from the ignition. He let out a long sigh and started to open the door before he caught motion outside the passenger-side window. It was Hayes, pulling her car into the spot next to him and waving with far too much energy given the hour.

"Hey," she said, practically leaping out of her car to walk beside him across the parking lot to the entrance. "Who was that hot cowboy with you last night?"

"Just a guy I know," Arch muttered, avoiding the full truth and an outright lie with one carefully constructed statement. He hated to lie and tried not to. He leaned in favor of just leaving out a few facts when he found it necessary to avoid the whole truth. He cast her a veiled look of irritation. "How is it that I had one beer and you had twelve, and I feel like I got dragged around the farm on the back of a surly bronc and you look like you had eighteen Starbucks this morning?"

"Like I could get Starbucks in this town," Erin said with a laugh. "Just takes some getting used to, Arch. Your resistance is low. The prescription is more drinking. You should come out tonight. Bring the cowboy."

"I don't think so," Arch said, back to all business—the business of covering up the crazy he'd witnessed and partaken in last night. "I have a feeling Hendricks—the cowboy—is busy. And you know, Alison was put off enough that I came dragging in as late as I did last night."

"You didn't tell her you were going out?" Erin gave him a curious look, a half-frown that said, *This is SO unlike you.*

"Didn't know I was," Arch said, treading close to the truth-line again. "I didn't expect to run into Hendricks."

"I was watching your conversation," Erin said as he opened the door for her. "You didn't look too happy with what he had to say," she suggested delicately.

Arch tried to decide whether to blow off her observation entirely or keep tap-dancing to avoid the truth. He ultimately landed somewhere in between. "You know how it is; sometimes people tell you things you don't really want to hear." It was true, and even somewhat applicable to the situation at hand.

She let it drop as they passed beyond the counter. As usual, there wasn't a soul in the waiting area, putting the lie to the name of the place. Behind the counter was a buzz of activity, though, or at least as much of a buzz as the Calhoun County Sheriff's Department ever got. Which was to say that the sheriff was clearly in his office, probably wrapping up after last night's patrol that he'd undertaken all by his lonesome, and a couple of the other guys were filling out paperwork they hadn't done the night before. Arch hadn't done his, either, and would have to take care of it before he headed out the door this morning, but first things came first. He grabbed his time card and punched in.

"Hey, Arch," Sheriff Reeve called from his office, "got a second?"

Arch felt a twinge of apprehension at being summoned into his boss's office, and let his long legs carry him thataway. After Reeve gestured for him to close the door and sit down, he did both, and sat there numbly, that odd feeling of dread hanging over him while Reeve leaned back in his chair, looking ridiculously relaxed and surprisingly alert for a man who'd done an overnight. "Got a call last night about some possible shots fired somewhere around the center of town," Reeve started. "Figured I'd check with you since you don't live too far off from there. You hear anything last night?"

Arch felt the tension fill him and tried to keep his face from puckering in reaction. "Near the center of town?" He tried for pensive and thought about praying that it would work. "Seems like that would have been something I'd have heard."

"Yeah," Reeve said, not looking too serious about the whole thing, "thought I'd ask you first. Came from the Widow Winslow that lives off First Ave, though, so I figured she might just be a little skittish about kids lighting off fireworks again. Not like it's the first time she's called in on some nuisance that turned out to be no big damned deal, you know?"

"Sure," Arch said. "Sorry I couldn't be more help." He felt as if he had a big sign proclaiming him a liar hanging over his head and wondered if the heat he felt in his face would give him away.

Reeve kind of squinted a frown at him, still back in his chair like it was a chaise or something, feet up on his desk. "Say, you doing all right? Everything okay with Alison?"

"Yeah," Arch said, almost fumbling it, but sticking the landing without stuttering. "She's still … you know, wanting a baby and all that."

Reeve gave a low chuckle. "You dog, you. Can't help but rub it in this old married man's face how much you're getting laid, can you? Well," he pointed a finger at Arch, "let me tell you something, newlywed. Your day will come. Sure, it's all hot and heavy now, in the beginning, but as time goes by and you start adding kids, those legs will close and you'll start to get laid on holidays and special occasions. Worse yet, you'll realize after a kid or three that really, that's about all you can handle." Reeve's gaze stayed centered on him the whole time, his cautionary tale just passing right over Arch. "Pretty soon you'll be over fifty, your hair will be all gone," he eyed Arch's nearly-shaven head, "which is maybe less of a concern for you than it was for me, but still—and that habit you've accumulated of getting laid only ever so often, it'll be permanent in your wife's eyes. So enjoy it while you can, cowboy."

Arch's ears perked up at the last part. "Excuse me?"

Reeve looked far-off for a second, then came back to Arch. "I said enjoy it while you can, because life gets busy and fucking tends to go by the wayside when kids start popping up. It's like the thing that screwing creates destroys its own genesis." Reeve seemed to ponder this for a moment. "Which, honestly, ain't unlike the kids themselves in what they do to their parents."

Arch tried to smile politely at this, nodding as though the Sheriff had unlocked one of the secrets of the universe to him.

"Oh, what the hell do you know," Reeve said, waving his hand at him dismissively. "I know that look, that nod. It's a, 'Sure, old man, but that shit won't ever happen to me.' Well, hot shot, I'm here to tell you that it will, but if you figure out how to avoid it without going outside your marriage, Mr. Hometown Hero, please tell us lesser mortals how to do it, will you? Spare a thought for the little guys?" Reeve wore a sidelong smile, with just enough sadness in it that Arch wanted to get the hell out of there rather than delve much deeper into it. "Have a good shift." Reeve gestured him away, gentler this time, and picked up a patrol report.

"You gonna get some sleep?" Arch said. He picked himself up out of the chair and heard his knee crack. It hurt a little bit, but not too much.

"Eventually," Reeve agreed. "Probably some this morning, before things get 'busy' this afternoon." He looked up from his paperwork and smiled. "Oh, and hey—I took a call from my wife this morning, something about calling out to the MacGruder dairy farm and not getting an answer. It's probably nothing, but your route takes you by there this afternoon, doesn't it?"

"Yeah," Arch agreed. It did, right out along Kilner Road, and he'd probably be past there before noon. "Want me to drop in and knock on the door, have them give her a call?"

"If you would," Reeve said. "And you're not too busy." He laughed. "As if you ever are in this county."

"I'll drop by," Arch said, stopping at the frame.

"Good," Reeve said and turned back to reading the report in his hand. "It's not like Old Man MacGruder to just drop off the face of the earth. He's way too ornery to just lay down and die."

*

Nothing ever went as it was fucking planned. Hollywood had gone to Chattanooga's version of a five-star hotel, something that was supposed to showcase Old-South charm and luxury, and they hadn't even had the fancy water in the squarish bottles from those islands in the Pacific that he couldn't remember the names of, ever. Not that it was important, but people looked at him funny when he tried to describe it to these ignorant savages. Fuck. In L.A. they would have fallen all over themselves trying to get him what he wanted, but when his egg white and spinach omelet showed up for breakfast, he had to argue with the dumb bitch who'd brought it up because she couldn't seem to get the fucking message.

"Well, I'm sorry, sir," she said, and she was red enough in the face that he believed she was sorry. Just not sorry enough to scour the fucking town to find him the water he was looking for.

"Look," he said, trying to be diplomatic after what had probably been the most epic bout of screaming he'd ever delivered, "I understand that your hotel and probably this whole town are just a little too backwoods to understand what kind of water I'm talking about. It's pure. It's clean. It's …" He searched for the right word. "It's elite. It's a cut above. So I can understand why you might not have heard of it down here—"

"I think they have some at the corner store," she said, still flushed. Her hair was dirty blond and she was freckled. Not homely, not compared to probably most people in this town, but she was ugly compared to the girls Hollywood was used to having on the casting couch. And fat. She was probably a size six. But not a terrible face, just not classic. He took a sip of the water she'd brought and avoided spitting it out in her face. Narrowly.

"I doubt they have my elite, cut-above-water at your fucking mom and pop convenience store," he said, biting back the snarl. He took a deep breath of air, realizing that the smell of cow shit was still with him, even after a shower. "This is so fucking ridiculous." His eyes alighted on hers. "How do you people live down here, like this? I bet you smoke a lot of pot just to get by."

"Um, no," she said, and there was a hint of wounded pride in how she said it. "I like it here."

He felt a lot of pity for her right then. "Well, aren't you a fucking simple little creature. I like that."

She flushed redder, which he wouldn't have thought possible with her farmer's complexion. "Other than this water problem—which I will try and solve—is there anything else I can get for you, sir?"

So she knew her place. She was pissed but biting it back. He owed her a smile, at least. "Just one thing. Maybe a couple things."

He managed to get her to stop screaming after only one good, long one.

*

Arch set the Explorer bumping down Kilner Road. It was gravel, "unimproved," as they called it sometimes when they were talking about paving roads that hadn't ever been paved. There wasn't much point to improving it, though, since only a half dozen people lived out here, and none of them cared that it was a gravel road. At least not enough to complain about it to the County Board of Supervisors.

He had the window down and the smell of the dairy farm wasn't too strong, yet. It'd get worse when he got closer, and the flies would get thicker. Arch had toured MacGruder's dairy farm sometime back in school, though he couldn't recall exactly when. Probably elementary school, back when things like cows were still exciting. He remembered the teachers saying Mr. MacGruder kept a pretty clean operation, unlike the big company farm closer to town. Being practically a one-man show, MacGruder probably took some pride in what he did. Arch wondered if that had slipped as MacGruder had aged because the white fence along the edge of the road was showing serious wear, the paint peeling off in long strips, revealing greyed wood beneath. Beyond was an empty field, no sign of cows, which were probably grazing at the backside of the property at this time of day.

Arch steered the Explorer into the drive, up toward the big white house, which was fading only a little less than the fences were. Beyond a little ways was the dairy barn off to his right, and straight ahead was a big metal gate about chest-high that kept the cows from wandering out of the fields and into MacGruder's driveway. The funny thing was, it was open. Arch frowned at that then shrugged it off, filing it away for later. It wasn't like there was a herd of cows wandering around out here, so they must be shut away in a field further up the hill. He settled his car into position behind MacGruder's old truck and got out, taking a long look around through his sunglasses.

His khakis didn't do much to defray the midday heat. This wasn't the hottest part of the day, even with the sun blazing overhead. That would come later, just about sunset, unbelievably. Still, it was hot, and Arch could feel his undershirt begin to stick with the first beads of sweat beneath his khaki uniform top. He was lucky in that at least he had short sleeves, but he would have seriously considered killing someone if it had meant he could wear shorts to work on a day like this. It brought him back to three-a-days, the murderous football practices his coach used to inflict when they were at camp in the summer. And southeastern Tennessee in the summer wasn't good picnicking weather, no sir.

Arch took in the MacGruder house with one long look. It was a fairly typical old southern style, with a porch that wrapped all the way around the thing. They had a couple rocking chairs up front, looked new, like maybe they'd been bought at Cracker Barrel in the last couple years. Nice woodwork. He'd thought about getting some, maybe when he had his own house instead of the little apartment.

He put that thought out of his mind as his shoes clomped up the short stairs to the screen door and he knocked on it good, three times. Old Man MacGruder was probably out in the fields, after all, and his wife was getting up there in the years. Better not chance her not hearing him. He gave the door one more good rap, then heard movement from inside, and saw a face appear from behind the curtain in the middle of the circular window in the door. When he caught sight of it—just a flash—he immediately that it was not a human face, with human eyes.

Arch took an involuntary step back, toward the edge of the porch, minding his footing, and drew his gun to low rest, pointed at a forty-five-degree angle down, the barrel on a trajectory to kneecap someone. It was a demon, he was damned near sure of it from that flash he'd seen behind the curtain, but when the door opened a moment later, he wasn't so sure.

"Krauther?" Arch asked, seeing the guy in the door frame. He hesitated, kept his gun low. He knew the guy, a good-for-nothing who had been that way for a long time. Had a half dozen disturbing-the-peace citations, had spent a few nights in the county jail.

"Hey, Arch," Krauther said, looking dark around the eyes. He was wearing a Metallica t-shirt and had a weak mustache across his upper lip, looking like a scrawny caterpillar had nested there after dipping itself in black ink. "What'd I do this time?"

"What are you doing in MacGruder's house?" Arch asked, keeping the gun out and low, ready to raise it and fire if necessary. Maybe he'd just seen things; active imagination, little sleep, and that cowboy had put him on edge, after all. Easy explanations were usually the closest to right. He'd known Krauther forever, for years, even before he became a sheriff's deputy. The guy was many things, criminal included, but a demon? Hard to believe.

"Oh, uh, yeah," Krauther said, looking every bit like the lying lowlife Arch knew him to be. He also looked tired, eyes drawn, like he'd been sleeping one off. "Old Man MacGruder hired me to do some work for him, you know, around the house. Me and some of the boys."

"Oh, yeah?" Arch scoured his memory for the names of the boys who ran with Krauther. "Who you got in there with you?"

Krauther tried to look innocent. Tried, but failed. "Just McGuire and Kellen." Both low-level, petty criminals as well.

"And Mrs. MacGruder?" Arch didn't stop staring at Krauther, looking for a sign of what he'd seen before, that flash from when he lifted the curtain and looked out.

"Oh, yeah, she's in here too," Krauther said. Another lie. A demon should be better at lying, shouldn't they? Not like a two-bit dumbass who'd had more brushes with the law over stupid things than anyone with half a brain ever should have.

How to play it, then? Arch only knew one way to handle things, and that was as close to the book as he could get while allowing for the possibility of demons, which weren't in the book. The rule book, at least. They were pretty clearly enumerated in the other book he read regularly, though. "I'm going to ask you to keep your hands visible and come out here and lay down on the driveway, Krauther. Your friends, too."

Krauther squinted at Arch, but in an unsurprised way. This wasn't his first arrest; he knew the score. "What for, Arch?"

"It's Deputy Stan to you, Krauther." He gestured once with his pistol, keeping it ready to be lifted and fire at Krauther if he got uppity. Unfortunately, Arch had seen what bullets did to the demon last night, which was to say nearly nothing. He was already frantically formulating a backup plan in case Krauther decided to try something. It mostly involved running.

"Deputy Stan is here to cuff us while he comes in and searches the house, boys," Krauther said, his hands still lazily resting on the frame and the door, spread between the two in an irritatingly casual show of unconcern. "What do we think of that?"

"I don't like it," Kellen said, appearing just off the porch to Arch's left. He was wearing shorts and a stained wife-beater shirt that might have been white once, many moons ago. Which was probably about the last time it'd been laundered. He had hair coming off his arms, his chest, sticking out from under the shirt in tufts.

"I don't think I wanna do that," McGuire said, appearing on the other side, up on the porch. "I don't like the feel of metal handcuffs against my skin. Not very sensuous."

"Yeah," Krauther said, pursing his lips and twisting the mustache with them. "I don't think we're coming with you today, lawman. The rules are fixing to change around here."

If Arch had been a swearing man, being at the center of a triangle of these three would have surely brought it out of him. As it was, he kept his cool, almost as much for lack of anything to say as any other reason. He knew they were demons, was sure of it now, and knew just as surely that shooting them in the face was unlikely to do much other than slow them down. In the absence of a neatly formed plan involving a sword that he could jab in their faces to cause them to be sucked back into whatever hell they came from, slowing them down was just about all he had. Even if these boys were human, they clearly meant him malice. They looked different, predatory, not like the small time losers they'd been before. He looked from Krauther to Kellen and wondered what had emboldened them.

Arch was normally restricted in the amount of violence he could use in a situation like this, but he was only a couple of percentage points away from one hundred percent certainty that these things were demons, so he gambled. He shot Krauther in the face three times.

Krauther staggered back, clearly not dead or missing his jaw. In fact, it made the demon face bleed through again, with a horrible scree'ing noise that chilled Arch's blood even in the hot summer sun. He snapped left and dealt with the next threat, shooting McGuire thrice in the chest for more than luck, and as the thing staggered from the shots, he turned and fired on Kellen, who was already coming up the porch steps. He actually knocked this one off his feet with the gunfire, dropping him onto the back of his neck on the ground. It didn't kill him, but it made him squirm and caused him to writhe, which was enough for Arch's plan to take effect.

He fired blind once more back at Krauther, who was starting to recover and come back at him, then Arch high-tailed it over Kellen's fallen form with an athletic leap and tore off for the Explorer. All three of them were back on their feet and running at him by the time he got the car started and into gear, and they'd just about caught him by the time he'd executed a roundabout in the drive. He floored it and doused the three of them with gravel as he shot out onto Kilner Road and left them in the dust as he cranked the speed up into the triple digits, trying to figure out what he could tell Sheriff Reeve about this whole mess.

*

Creampuff watched the whole thing go down, Ygrusibas whispering to her the whole time. It was nothing more than a curiosity to old Creampuff, chewing grass as she watched the tall, dark-skinned man in the dirt-colored uniform talking to three of the beasts that had eaten her farmer. *Demons,* Ygrusibas said as the thing in the doorway had yelled for his fellows and she'd seen them come out on either side of the uniformed man. She kept chewing, though, no reason to be that concerned.

He knows, Ygrusibas said to her as the dark-skinned man started making loud noises with the wand in his hand, and the demons started falling, falling and hurting, she knew, like that time she'd brushed up against the metal fence in the far pasture. The uniformed man made a hurried run and went back to his moving building, and it thundered off with the three demons in pursuit.

He's dangerous, Ygrusibas told her, and Creampuff nodded, though it was in time with her jaw moving to chew the grass. Food was a higher priority to her than the uniformed man, after all. Food was more important than anything.

NO, the voice told her, this thing that was so loud, so commanding, this thing that swore it could make her hurt worse than the fence in the far pasture. She doubted that as the fence was very painful. *Nothing is more important than Ygrusibas.*

Creampuff didn't want to argue with that, so she didn't. She just kept chewing and watched the moving building with the uniformed man in it speed off down the road behind the fence. She nodded along with Ygrusibas, though, just in case. What else was she supposed to do about it?

Chapter 4

Hendricks awoke to a pounding on the door that was almost perfectly matched to the pounding in his head. He was disoriented, and for a moment he thought he was back in New Orleans, on a dock, waking up for what seemed like the first time, bright sunlight streaming into his eyes.

It turned out that the sunlight was coming from behind the curtains, which were drawn but had an imperfect seam where the two met and were letting in outside illumination. Which would have been fine, if not for the pounding in Hendricks's head. "Just a minute," he said, realizing it was someone at the door. The stale air of the motel was heavy in the room, and it was already hot, the air conditioning fighting a losing battle against the Tennessee summer. He struggled into his boxers, the sweat on his body and the throbbing ache in his skull and somewhere much lower making the fit more difficult than it needed to be. The hammering sound at the door came again, relentless this time, and he shouted, "Hold your goddamn horses, I'm coming," as he pulled on his jeans.

When he pulled open the door a minute later, after closing his eyes from the blinding burst of light, he managed to wrench them open to find Deputy Arch staring at him, looking a little nonplussed to his admittedly hungover eyes. "What the fuck is it?" he asked, more than a little nonplussed himself.

The deputy's level of tension was clearly higher than his because the man just barged in, bumped past him and into the room, ignoring the fact that Hendricks didn't even have a shirt on yet. He caught a whiff of himself as he started to close the door and realized that showering hadn't been on the list of things to do before he'd passed out last night, apparently. And it probably wouldn't have made a difference because the air conditioner wasn't doing shit to alleviate the heat in the room, and he was already covered with a thin sheen of perspiration. He closed the door and stared at Arch's uniformed back as he stood in the middle of his room. "Well, what?

It's a little too early in the morning to be paying a courtesy call, but you ain't slapped cuffs on me yet—"

"It's afternoon," Arch said, turning to face him. The man looked beleaguered, to say the least. Spooked would be another way to say it. He was sweating, and Hendricks got the feeling it wasn't just from the heat.

"Sorry," Hendricks said, not really apologizing so much as being polite. "It was a late night and I had way more to drink than you." He brushed past Arch and found his soiled t-shirt on the counter next to the sink and put it on. "What brings you to my door at this hour?" He flinched a little. "Which admittedly is more unholy to me than to you, I suppose."

"Demons," Arch said.

Hendricks just let that lie there for a minute, waiting to see if he'd elaborate. "What about 'em?"

"They're here," Arch said, like that explained everything.

"Yes, I know that," Hendricks said mildly. If this was what he'd been awakened for, the lawman was lucky he had a badge. If he'd just been some schmoe, like an IT help desk worker, Hendricks would have flattened him with a punch to the jaw for this shit. Especially if he'd been an IT help desk worker. Smug, unhelpful fucks. "It's why I'm here."

"No, I mean," Arch said, shaking his head like he could shake it into making sense, "I went out on a call from my boss, a— not a missing person, exactly, but like a friend who they couldn't reach—anyway, I go up to the door and there are these good ol' boys I know from way back. Stupid guys, real idiots, three or four misdemeanors each, maybe a petty felony or so apiece, and they're hanging out in these people's house." His hands were moving when he talked, like an Italian. Hendricks tried to hide his amusement because clearly the big man had been rattled by what he'd seen. "I swear, when one of them peered out of the curtain at me, I—I *saw* him."

Hendricks waited to see if it was a pause in the conversation that Arch was using to take a breath. After another moment it was pretty clear he was waiting for a response, so Hendricks spoke. "Yes, that's generally what would happen when someone stares out at you through a window, you would see them."

"No," Arch said, head shaking again, "I mean I *saw* him. Saw him saw him. Like his demon face."

Hendricks felt an ashy sensation, like he'd swallowed something he shouldn't have. Which he had, but he didn't think it was the beer doing this to him. "Look," he said, trying to be sympathetic, "what I told you last night, maybe it's got you kind of rattled. It's not like everybody's a demon, okay? Even in a hotspot, they're pretty few and far between. Most people are just honest citizens—or citizens, at least—and if you saw these guys getting into trouble, the odds are good that they're probably just the petty criminals you were describing, no demonic influence necessary—"

"So then they tried to surround me and I shot each of them in the face and ran."

"Oh, fuck!" Hendricks was already cursing himself for his stupidity. Explain the demon world to someone for the first time in five years, and the next day they go and commit multiple homicides … "Look, those guys … they probably weren't demons …" He felt like shit and not just because of the hangover. Were these his fault? It felt a little like they were.

"Well, they chased me down the driveway after three head shots each," Arch said, his eyes were burning. The man was pissed, deeply so. "I would say that unless you know a lot of petty criminals that can take a few .40 rounds between the eyes and then catch up to a car doing thirty—"

"Oh, shit, you ran into demons!" Hendricks said.

"Yes, that's what I've been trying to tell you," Arch said, well, archly. Hendricks couldn't blame him.

"Sorry, I thought maybe you were just a little overzealous," Hendricks said. "You know, first day after I turned your world upside down, thought maybe you were still acclimating. I know my first day after learning about demons, I was seeing them everywhere, looking in everybody's eyes trying to figure out if they were one. I'm told it's a natural response, especially when you've witnessed something traumatic involving—" He shut his mouth and bore the scrutiny of Arch's curious and furious stare while he pondered how best to change the track of the conversation. "Where were they?" That was easy.

"Old Man MacGruder's dairy farm," Arch said. He seriously was pissed, like these demons had called his mother a whore or something. "Three of them that I saw."

"This MacGruder a friend of yours?" Hendricks asked with more than a little curiosity of his own.

"What?" Arch said, like it was a question out of the blue. "No, I barely knew the man. What do we do now?"

"We?" Hendricks asked, a little dumbfounded. "I don't know what we do, but I'm gonna try and go out there and kill them in a bit. Might have to get a little breakfast first, though." He patted his stomach, felt the rumble of displeasure. "Or maybe not." He tapped on his forehead then stopped when it hurt. "How many of them did you say there were?"

"Three."

Hendricks got a pained look that wasn't just from how he was feeling. "Shit." He waited for a beat, thinking it over. "Okay, maybe this *is* a 'we' thing instead of a 'me' thing."

*

Arch didn't love the thought of involving Hendricks, a near-stranger, in what was really department business. But when a demon hunter wanders into town the day before you nearly get overrun with demons, it narrows your options right down: either tell the people around you that you think there are unearthly creatures involved in unpleasant dealings in your town or go to the supposed professional about them. Part of Arch was wondering if Hendricks was jerking him around, but it seemed mighty unlikely. The cowboy was leaned against the door of Arch's patrol car, looking like he was suffering just from being up and moving, and mighty displeased to be awake even now. "You gonna be all right?" Arch asked him.

"I'll manage," Hendricks came back.

They rode along toward Kilner Road in silence, Arch not really wanting to say much of anything, on account of how pissed and suspicious he still was, and Hendricks staying quiet, Arch assumed, because he was still hung over. Arch didn't know that he'd ever been as hungover as Hendricks was now, and he reckoned he'd be pretty okay with going to his grave without ever knowing how it felt, thank you very much.

"It's down here," Arch said as they turned on Kilner Road. "Got a plan?"

Hendricks sat up in interest. "Where there's three, there's a possibility of more."

Arch watched Hendricks unbuckle his seat belt and lean forward to look down the road. "How many can you take at once?"

Hendricks appeared to consider this for a moment, while still staring down the road. "Three, maybe, depending on what kind they are. While I'm fighting two of them, though, the third will probably be killing you, since you don't really have a good way to hold them at bay."

"Bad plan," Arch pronounced. "I veto that one."

"Agreed," Hendricks said, and motioned for Arch to stop the car. "It's pretty sub-optimal. Anything head-on is, really. I think we should make this a reconnaissance mission, take a look around, see what we can see, and be ready to hoof it on back to the car at the first sign of trouble." Arch had drawn the car to a stop on the side of the road and Hendricks opened the door, letting the summer heat seep in, humidity and all. "I doubt they're gonna be going anywhere, and it ain't like they're up to much here. It's a dairy farm, after all, not a chemical weapons factory." The cowboy sniffed and then made a face. "Well, maybe …"

"They're up to murder, in all likelihood," Arch said tightly, and his hand went to his pistol. He ejected the magazine and checked to make sure it was topped off again. He carried spare bullets in a gym bag in the hatch back of the Explorer, and he'd filled it up before picking up Hendricks at the motel. He listened to the satisfying click as he pushed the magazine back into the Glock and then opened the back of the car and pulled out a shotgun, too. When Hendricks gave him the *What-the-hell-is-that-for* look he just said, "it may not kill them, but it seems like it hurts them, and it for sure puts 'em down for a few seconds."

"True enough," Hendricks said, and they were heading for the fence.

"Careful," Arch said, pointing at the low wire. "It's electrified."

"I suspected as much," Hendricks said, easing over it after using the second wire as a brace to land his big cowboy boot. "Being from Wisconsin, I've been in a cow pasture or two." He gave Arch a grin, this one pretty real.

"Y'all ain't got much else for entertainment up there, huh?" Arch pondered what to do about the shotgun before finally just handing it over to Hendricks and keeping an eye on the man until he got over the fence and got it handed back to him.

"I think that's the North's joke for the South." Hendricks squinted. "Actually, that's mostly our joke for Iowa. We don't think of much south of that or Illinois."

They made their way through a copse of trees just past the fence. It was a grove of pines, tall ones, with rough patches of bark that made it look like each tree was patterned like a turtle shell. The thick smell of them in the heat wasn't quite overwhelming, but it did make Arch long for a nap. By the look of him, Hendricks was feeling the same, though for different reasons. Instead, they were sneaking up on a passel of demons that were hiding out in a dairy farmer's house. A thought occurred to Arch. "Do you think Old Man MacGruder is still alive?"

Hendricks didn't halt his walk, but he did look back from where he was leading the way. "That the guy that owns the place?"

"Yeah."

"He's dead," Hendricks said, his voice flat. "Demons aren't big on hostages or prisoners." He waited a second then spoke again. "I shouldn't say that—there are some species of demons that are big on prisoners, but only because they like their food fresh. Like, really fresh. Basically live and still squirming while they eat it."

Arch felt his grip tighten on the shotgun. "These things … they eat people?"

"Some of them, yeah." Hendricks kept on going, kept his stride. "Sometimes only certain parts, depending on what kind of demon they are—you know, eyes, noses, butt cheeks. Sometimes it's a specific cut of meat, like the human version of the sirloin or some shit like that. Some will just eat the intangibles, like your soul." He looked back and Arch knew by the dark look on Hendricks's face he wasn't bullshitting. "Some don't eat people, and they're peaceable enough, integrated into human society without a hitch. I don't run across many of those, but there's probably a reason for that."

Arch chewed on that thought as they came upon a slight rise. "The house is just up over there." He pointed the shotgun up over the hill and Hendricks stopped. "We might ought to creep low, just in case they're watching out the windows."

"These guys seem like the cautious type to you?" Hendricks was asking sort of seriously, but there was a twinkle of mischief in his eyes.

"They're pretty dumb as humans, but now that I know they're demons, I'm a little more concerned."

"Fair enough," Hendricks said and crouched down, the long trail of his drover coat dipping to the ground with him. Arch squatted next to him. "Let's get up over there and—"

Hendricks didn't get a chance to finish his sentence before Arch felt the shotgun being ripped from his grasp. It hit him squarely across the nose and he saw stars, then the hard metal barrel was pressed tight against his neck, squeezing the breath out of him. He struggled for breath, and as his eyes fell on Hendricks, he saw the cowboy with Kellen's hairy forearm across his neck, choking him out exactly the same as was happening to him. He started to pass out, the bright sunny sky fading as he felt his strength drain, sagging against the strong arms that were holding him so tightly that even Arch couldn't seem to find a way to fight back.

Chapter 5

Hendricks didn't love the smell of the demon that had grabbed him and couldn't see much of him other than a hairy arm that had him around the neck in a way that locked his throat. He could see that Arch was getting it even worse, being choked out by some fucker in a button-up shirt that had grease smudged all over it. The smell of the dairy farm was thick in the air around him, and a lone fly buzzed past Hendricks's face as the son of a bitch who had him around the neck started dragging him.

"You're … choking him … to death," Hendricks managed, catching the attention of the grubby fuck who had Arch, shotgun across his neck.

The guy with the button-up readjusted, letting the shotgun loose from around Arch's neck and grabbing him one-armed, holding him about like the other guy had Hendricks. It wasn't pretty, but demons had the strength to keep a human down with only one arm in the fight. Hendricks hadn't really expected his warning about choking Arch to death to do much more than produce a guffaw and was surprised when it actually stopped the guy. He even looked concerned, or his human facade did, anyway. That made Hendricks curious, because the idea of a demon concerned with a human's welfare was laughable, at least on the surface. His mind immediately ran to the idea that something else was going on, something that they needed the two of them for—alive. Which was worrisome.

"You okay?" he asked Arch, whose eyes were rolling back in his head. There was a coughing fit from the big man, and it would have been surreal to see the six-foot-two mountain of a deputy manhandled by some scrub fuck who looked like he'd stumbled out from between the gears of a machine—if not for the fact that the one who was manhandling him was a demon. Hendricks wasn't sure what kind, though, because he'd yet to see the real face of the thing.

"Still breathing," Arch answered him after a horrendous coughing fit. The grubby bastard who was dragging him along had the shotgun, and was paying no attention to Arch's hands. Probably wasn't very concerned he'd do something untoward, because presently Arch was doing everything he could just to keep from having his head pulled off as he was dragged along. That might change, though. Hendricks was in much the same boat, trying to keep up with the hairy bastard that was pulling him along headfirst. He didn't want to go for his sword until he knew the demon was well and truly distracted, though, because even if he pulled it and struck true before the bastard could rip his head off—which was iffy—it was almost certain that Arch's demon would kill him plenty dead before Hendricks could get the man free.

They were pulled along unwillingly over the hill. The flies were thicker now, and Hendricks saw the pastureland with the wide open fields from their slightly elevated perch. He tried to ignore the pain in his neck from being dragged along by the fucker who had him, but it was hard to dismiss. Harder still to resist pulling his sword and shoving it right up the bastard's ass. He was pretty well positioned for that, anyway.

"Hey, Kellen," the one dragging Arch said, "ain't this supposed to be a dairy farm, man?"

"Yeah," the hairy one who had the back of Hendricks's neck buried in his armpit replied, "so what?"

"Well, why ain't there any cows, man?"

Kellen paused, letting Hendricks brush up against his hairy side. "Well, there's one." He pointed, but Hendricks couldn't see it very well, since he was doing it with the other hand, the one that wasn't currently jammed against Hendricks's windpipe.

There was a pause, and the one holding Arch seemed to think about this. "Isn't that the same one we saw last night?"

"Yep," Kellen agreed.

"So," the other said, "shouldn't there be more than one around here?"

"I dunno," Kellen said, plainly uninterested in the affairs of dairy farming. "Who cares? They're cows. They're probably here somewhere."

Hendricks might have given that some more thought, but it wasn't a pressing concern for him, waiting as he was for a fine opportunity to turn the tables on the two stooges without getting Arch killed. He was all about saving his own neck, but he thought he'd feel more than a little poorly about it if his bid for freedom cost the life of the deputy. There was something to be said for not throwing your comrades to the wolves, metaphorically speaking, and Arch was as close as he had to one of those. Hell, Arch was one of the few people who'd actually had a conversation with him in the last few years. It was probably bad when you could count the number of people you talked to for more than thirty seconds in any given month on one hand.

"We need to take these boys to Hollywood," Kellen said.

"No, thanks," Hendricks gasped, struggling for air, "I hate California."

"Look," the hairy one said, grinding his wrist into Hendricks's neck. This time Hendricks saw what he was pointing at. It was a sedan, kinda fancy, pulling in the driveway. They got dragged down the hill as someone wearing a sleeveless flannel shirt came running around the side and opened the back door to allow a man to step out. If Hendricks thought the car was fancy, it was nothing compared to the guy riding in the back.

He was medium sized, with a ponytail and slicked back hair. He wore an earring, an opulent little thing that Hendricks could see sparkle with diamonds. He was a white guy, wearing a grey suit that reeked of money. Hendricks had heard someone say one time that you couldn't always tell when a suit was expensive, but he was pretty sure this one was because it seemed to fit its wearer just about perfectly. He wore sunglasses, too, one of the more expensive types. All the fancy accouterments aside, Hendricks got the sense that this guy, Hollywood, was a full-flow douchenozzle, an impression that was confirmed the minute the bastard opened his mouth.

"What the fuck is this?" Hollywood asked as Hendricks and Arch were dragged into view. "Where did you find these peckerwoods?"

"Up over the hill," Kellen said. "Heard 'em parking the car down the road a ways when we were out in the woods for a smoke."

Hendricks didn't smell cigarettes on either one of them, and Hollywood looked at them funny for a moment but let it pass. "Well," Hollywood said and broke into a smile, "I guess that saves us the trouble of looking for sacrifices for tonight." He pulled the sleeve of his suit up and looked at a glittering gold watch beneath. "Now we just have to figure out what to do with them for the next few hours."

"So you're Hollywood?" Hendricks said, causing his handler to try and adjust his chokehold again to shut him up. "Let me guess … you're a big fan of Hulk Hogan during the NWO years?"

Hollywood didn't blink, just looked at him over the sunglasses for about a quarter second before shifting his gaze away. "Can you put them in the farmer's cellar?"

"I don't like the deputy," the sleeveless one called out, keeping his distance from Arch and Hendricks. Which was good. It meant he couldn't react immediately when Hendricks started some shit in a minute. Hendricks' coat was dragging on the ground, billowing around him, which was also good. Plainly none of them had seen his sword yet.

"I don't like you, either, Munson," Arch said, struggling to get the words out.

Hollywood looked over his shades between Arch and Munson. "Little animosity here?"

"I had to let him arrest me last year," Munson said, rubbing one of his tan, sleeveless arms. The red and black flannel shirt looked ridiculous, all the more so because of how damned hot it was outside. "Wasn't gentle about it."

"He arrested all of us last year, dumbass," Kellen said. "McGuire and I," he nodded to the one holding Hendricks, "spent six months in the lockup in Ferguson together after that little debacle."

"Boys shoulda kept to your parole," Arch said, not struggling to do anything but remain upright against the hold of a demon-man that looked like he weighed a hundred and twenty at most, compared to Arch's easy two-twenty. If he'd been a man and not a demon, Hendricks would have bet the deputy could have beat the fuck out of him and twelve others like him at the same time.

"Can we kill him when it comes time?" Kellen asked Hollywood. He wore a stupid grin, and Hendricks did not like the look of it. Not at all. It reeked of impatience, and made him think that maybe Arch wouldn't make it to whenever this ritual sacrifice was going to happen.

"No," Hollywood said simply, and all the air went right out of that discussion. Hendricks paid a little attention to the subtle nuance of the reactions that showed; even though these demons only wore veneers of humanity, they were complete. Emotion definitely showed through on the faces, which was just another thing Hendricks didn't understand about how these fuckers managed to look human even on the surface. Mostly. "I need them alive, and I need to do the sacrificing."

"Well, can we rough him up some?" The sleeveless one—Munson—asked.

Hollywood seemed to ponder this question, and he took his time. About ten seconds later, he said, "No. I don't need them flawless, but I don't trust you boys to know human beings enough to keep from killing them in your enthusiasm." He gave a light shrug and let the sunglasses drop back over his eyes. "You can eat them when I'm done, though."

"Well," Hendricks said, drawing their attention to him, "I think I've heard just about all I need to hear of this."

"Oh, yeah?" Hollywood said with dark amusement. "Is that so?"

"It's so," Hendricks said.

Hollywood adopted an air of true interest in what Hendricks was saying, even over the distance between them. Hendricks could practically feel the condescending fake concern from the demon, and it pissed him off even more. "What are you going to do about it?" Like Hendricks was the most inconsequential insect to ever cross his path.

"Quite a bit, actually," Hendricks said.

"Oh?" Hollywood said, with a snicker. "How?"

"I don't know if you noticed this," Hendricks said, not bothering to squirm, just letting Kellen hold him tight around the neck, "but you didn't exactly hire the most capable cowhands on the ranch—metaphorically speaking, of course."

Hollywood glared at him from behind the sunglasses, and Hendricks saw a little bit of the demon fire within. It didn't stop him, though. Hollywood started to say something smartass back, but Hendricks bucked his head down, dropping his cowboy hat down and catching it with his left hand while dragging his right into his belt and snagging the hilt of his sword. He drew it and lobbed it, slow, hilt first, right at Arch, who was watching him.

The minute Hendricks had his right hand free of the sword, he thrust it into his cowboy hat, like he was going to pull a rabbit out of it. Which he was—again, metaphorically speaking. His hand caught the handle of the switchblade hidden in the brim for emergencies just such as this and he flipped the blade open as he pulled it clear of the hat. He felt Kellen snugging his grip tighter in preparation to hurt him, but he thrust the knife up and into the base of Kellen's neck, dragging forth an unearthly scream that was cut short as a hot wind blew Hendricks a step forward.

The whole area was quiet, just for a second as Hendricks saw the demon gripping Arch dissolve into his own burst of blackness and fire. The big lawman staggered back to his feet across from Hendricks, the weight of the demon off his back, sword gripped tightly in one hand and shotgun back in the other.

"That's what I was gonna do," Hendricks said to Hollywood, who just stood glaring at him quietly, Munson at his shoulder looking ready to jump the two of them. Hendricks just put the cowboy hat back on his head and clutched the switchblade tighter in his hand, keeping it pointed at the two of them that were remaining.

Hollywood didn't say anything for a minute, then calmly took off his glasses and folded them up, slipping them into the breast pocket of his suit. "You boys are in over your head here," Hollywood said then cringed and looked to Arch almost apologetically. "I didn't mean 'boy' in an offensive way, in your case." He glared back at Hendricks. "In yours, I hope offense was taken."

Hendricks looked at him with complete disbelief. "Are you shitting me?"

"I wouldn't shit you," Hollywood said, "at least not around here. There's too much of it already lying on the ground. I just don't want anyone thinking I'm racist."

"You were just talking about killing us a minute ago," Hendricks said.

"Oh, I'm still going to kill you—both of you," Hollywood said with a wide grin. "Just want to make sure we understand there's no racial animosity to it."

Hendricks had to stop himself from asking if the douchenozzle was fucking kidding again. He hated repeating himself. Instead, he decided to probe a little toward the other thing Hollywood had said. "In over our heads, huh?"

"So over your heads," Hollywood said with a sappy grin. "I could tear the heads from your bodies right now with minimal effort—"

The *BOOM!* of a shotgun going off would have drowned out whatever Hollywood was going to say next, even if it hadn't blown him off his feet and bounced him off the car to come to rest face-down in the mud. The second round of buckshot hit Munson, and his sleeveless ass took a dive as well. Hendricks didn't wait for them to get ambitious; he pulled the .45 out of his belt and blasted the tires of Hollywood's sedan with a shot each, then blew out the front tire of MacGruder's old truck for good measure. That was all the cars he could see in the drive, and he figured it'd slow these idiots down. He popped Munson in the head with a .45 round for good measure then took off at a run back toward the woods, only a step behind Arch, who'd apparently gotten to same smart idea to haul ass back to the patrol car.

"How fast can they run?" Arch asked, running a hell of a lot faster than Hendricks. Hendricks poured it on, trying to keep the distance from widening too much. The hill wasn't too bad, but it would have been easier if Hendricks hadn't been holding the knife and the gun. Arch had a long sword and a shotgun in his hands, though, and they didn't seem to be slowing him down at all.

"Fast enough to catch us if they're of a mind," Hendricks said. "Might want to keep that shotgun handy to pepper them if they come up on us too quick."

Arch slowed and cast a wary eye back, letting Hendricks catch him. Arch cleared the fence like a hurdler and Hendricks was a step behind him, managing to keep his footing while using the wires to step up, and when they reached the car, Arch already had it moving as Hendricks got in and slammed the door. They would have peeled out if it hadn't been a gravel road. Instead they flung enough dust in the air to bring to Hendricks's mind the time he'd been in Arizona when a dust storm blew through. Except that time he'd been fighting a demon in someone's back yard when it happened. He thought about it for a second more. It was almost exactly like that time, actually.

*

It took Hollywood a few minutes to pull himself up from the mud. Not because he was hurt, but because his ten thousand dollar Savile Row suit that he bought in London had holes all over the front of it. He thought about crying, but one of his minions was still out there. It'd be a bad leadership example.

"Boss?" Sleeveless asked. Hollywood knew his name was Munson now, but he would always think of him as Sleeveless, because it was just as real of a name to the thug as Munson was. "Boss, you want me to chase after them?"

"No," Hollywood said after a moment. "They're ready for that, ready to fight. Let them go for now. It's not even close to midnight yet, and we'll have plenty of time between now and then to sneak up and surprise the hell out of them. Divide and conquer, you know? Hell, even if they hang out together between now and then … you know what?" Hollywood felt a sneer coming on. "Even if I had to put this whole ritual off for a day, it might be worth it to slaughter them in a way that Ygrusibas would find palatable. It's not like the ritual is specific about how they have to die. Maybe Ygrusibas is looking for something showier, like feeding them their own intestines. Beating them to death with their own forearms, you know, something eye-catching." Hollywood slipped out of the shredded remnants of his suit coat, almost cringing at the damage. That suit had closed a few deals for him. He looked back to the woods, where the two pains in his ass had disappeared. Now the ones who'd fucked it up were going to close a big deal for him. The biggest, really. There was some sort of symmetry in that. He turned to Sleeveless.

"So … got any other friends in town?"

*

Creampuff watched through the fence as the two men got the better of four demons and ran off. Ygrusibas wanted to do something about it, but there wasn't much Creampuff could do, really. Creampuff was feeling awfully bloated anyway, thanks to Ygrusibas and his helpful suggestions.

The smell of cow dung wasn't something Creampuff objected to, being around it on a near-constant basis, but now it had turned different, at least in the last few hours. Creampuff could barely stand the smell of herself, but that was becoming less and less important as Ygrusibas was taking more and more control of the proceedings. Creampuff had never cared for the taste of meat before, not that she'd had much chance to eat it. But now, she was eating tons of it. Literally tons. Every other cow in the herd was dead, consumed by Creampuff, and all on the order of Ygrusibas. The skeletons were just over the hill, but now that it was done, Creampuff was stuck in the front part of the pasture, watching the goings-on, waiting for the strength of Ygrusibas to kick in, so she could finally be rid of that accursed gate, finally walk out of this confinement into the world, and—

There was a patch of grass to her right, and it looked pretty good, so she dipped her head to get at it. Ygrusibas sighed, somewhere within. This was not exactly going the way it had hoped it would.

*

Arch wasn't all that happy about running away from the MacGruder place twice in the same day. It felt like failure, like losing, and he'd never liked the taste of that—on the football field or off. "Damn," he said, feeling the knuckles crack as he tightened his grip on the steering wheel.

"We made it out alive," Hendricks said from the passenger seat, still breathing hard as they turned from Kilner back onto the paved road. "That counts for something. And did you catch the whiff off that Hollywood guy? I smelled power."

"I smelled cow dung."

"Well, yeah, that too," Hendricks agreed. "But Hollywood was clearly the brains of that operation. And he wasn't like the others. They were lessers—"

"Define 'lessers,'" Arch said. One of the 'lessers,' as Hendricks was calling them, had nearly rung the life out of him without much effort. If these were the lessers, he didn't want to be around for the greaters.

"Lesser demons," Hendricks said, as though it were the most natural thing in the world. Arch supposed after living this stuff for years, maybe it was natural. Not to him, though. Not yet. "This Hollywood is planning some sort of a ritual that includes human sacrifice." Now Hendricks was just musing out loud, looking out the windshield, and Arch wondered if the man even knew he was still there. "Not good, not good …"

"No," Arch said, "human sacrifice is not good. You think that's what happened to the MacGruders?"

"Huh?" Hendricks looked startled, like Arch had just called him back from some place of deep thought. "Oh, yeah, probably. I mean, unless it was some sort of group sacrifice, and he needed more. Yeah, he probably killed them already." He frowned. "What kind of a ritual needs multiple sacrifices? What kind of a ritual can you pause right in the middle and go get more sacrifices?"

Part of Arch wanted to let him just muse it out until he had it figured. It was not the same part that worked for the Sheriff's Department and needed answers to go with this annoying mystery that had washed up in his town from somewhere south of hell. "Are there a lot of these sort of rituals done?"

Hendricks gave an equivocal left-to-right bob of his head. "Some, mostly in hotspots. Demons have all sorts of rituals, praying to greater demons than themselves for fortune, luck, fame—"

"Fame?" Arch looked at Hendricks skeptically. "What does a demon want with fame?"

"Half the cast of every show on reality TV are demons," Hendricks answered. "More if you're watching MTV."

Arch thought that one over for a minute. "Makes sense."

"Anyway," Hendricks went on, "there's lots of reasons for a demon to do a ritual. They do them all the time. Most are innocuous and involve pretty innocent components. Maybe cadaver parts at worst, greenery at best. Something involving human sacrifice, though …" He frowned, deeply. "Doesn't sound too good. That's pretty far out of my league, though."

"Of course it is," Arch said, and he knew he was strained because he was being sarcastic, "because we couldn't have all the answers just conveniently at hand."

"It would make things a little more boring," Hendricks said with a smile. "I have someone I can call for help, but she's a little tough to get ahold of. I've also got a couple books I can read through, see if there might be any specifics in there."

"What about this Hollywood guy and the other two demons?" Arch tried to keep his eye on the ball.

"I only saw one other."

"There were two before," Arch said. "Munson wasn't there when I showed up the first time, Krauther was the one who answered the door." He paused. "I wonder where he was."

"Doesn't matter," Hendricks said. "I'm concerned about that Hollywood guy. I don't think he's a lesser."

Arch didn't care for that assessment, either. "Can you kill a … what would he be then, a greater?"

"Might be," Hendricks said. "Might be worse."

Nope. Arch didn't like the sound of that at all.

"Fifteen," came Erin's voice out of his car radio, "this is Dispatch."

Arch wanted to curse but didn't. Instead he thumbed the mike. "This is Fifteen, go ahead, Dispatch."

"We have reports of a black SUV weaving around out near the interstate. What's your twenty, over?" Harris's voice was alert.

"I'm heading that way right now," Arch replied. "Fifteen out." He hung up the mike without another word. He knew a moment later it was brusque, especially for him, but he had other things on his mind.

Hendricks waited about five seconds before speaking. "Was that that Erin girl we ran into at the bar last night?"

Arch looked at him sidewise. They'd just been set upon by a pack of demons who were sacrificing human beings and the cowboy wanted to make time? "Yeah."

Hendricks just nodded, like he was assimilating that piece of information for later. He waited another minute before he spoke again. "She got a boyfriend?"

Arch sent him a look that was beyond pointed. "You serious?"

Hendricks shrugged, trying to deflect it. "This is what I do, you know."

"Like a job you go home from every day?" Arch asked, still letting loose the heat. "It's life and death for the rest of us. At least it seems like it was for MacGruder and his wife."

"Isn't your job life and death?" Hendricks asked, and Arch didn't look at him. "Pretty sure I've heard of cops killed in the line of duty."

"Not around here," Arch said tightly.

"You could die any time," Hendricks said, voice sounding awfully far away. "Life's a serious business, if you want to be serious about it all the time. You could be walking down the street in New Orleans with your wife and get set upon by demons, killed, and tossed into the harbor." He gave Arch a sidelong look of his own. "Yeah, killing demons can be serious. I've been pretty serious about it for a long time. Made it more than a job, I made it into something I was called to do." He rubbed his face, like there was some way to get the tired look off of it. "Been wondering lately if I've been a little too serious about it."

Arch waited, thinking over what had just been said. "That didn't actually happen to you, did it?" He didn't look at Hendricks, but could see him in his peripheral vision. "That thing in New Orleans?"

Hendricks took a minute to answer, and he wasn't convincing. "I'm still here, aren't I?"

Arch decided to let it go. "I gotta drop you off and go look for some dumb sonofagun that's not able to find a designated driver to keep his stupid self from weaving all over the road. What's the next move?"

"I'll do some research," Hendricks said. "Demon rituals usually happen under cover of night." He chewed his lip as he thought. "I'm not loving the thought of assaulting the farm again, especially not at night, when those guys are at their strongest."

"If we don't stop them," Arch said, "they're gonna grab some other poor bastard and throw them into the hot seat we were supposed to be in tonight, right?"

Hendricks didn't have to think long about that one. "Probably."

Arch gritted his teeth to keep from swearing. It was an old habit and seemed likely to come in handy in the immediate future. "How do we stop them?"

Hendricks gave that some thought. "I don't know." He didn't sound too down about it, more resigned. "If that guy Hollywood is as badass as he looks like he is, I don't know that we can."

Chapter 6

Hendricks wasn't a fan of being a bearer of bad news, and Arch didn't take it too well, either. They turned on the main stretch through town and thc tall man said nothing as they beelined toward the interstate. "We just put a pretty hurting on him, killed two of his thugs," Arch said, breaking the silence. "Why would you think we can't take this Hollywood guy out?"

"We got lucky with the thugs," Hendricks answered patiently, remembering he was instructing someone with no experience in the demon world. "They were slow and stupid; they should have broken our necks before we could have even gotten our hands on our weapons. They didn't, and the fact that you blew off a couple shotgun rounds at Hollywood and Munson helped our cause a lot. But he was playing possum, I'm telling you. He didn't need to stay down as long as he did, he should have been up on his feet and after us in hot pursuit. The fact that he wasn't is worrisome."

"You gonna worry about it?" Arch asked.

"Maybe later," Hendricks said. "Anyway, if he's a greater, we're not just talking about the power to choke us out in seconds, we're talking about the ability to rip a human body apart with his bare fingers in just a couple of eyeblinks. I've seen whole teams of demon hunters wiped out by greaters, and we're talking people with serious experience."

"What about the shotgun?" Arch didn't want to let it go, apparently. "I put them both down with it."

"Guns can be helpful as a delaying tactic against demons," Hendricks said. "But they don't have enough force to be able to break through the veneer of their human forms, which is what you need to have happen to let their essence leak out and get swallowed back up into hell."

"You telling me you can stab with that sword harder than a bullet can hit?" Arch plainly didn't believe that either.

"No," Hendricks said with a grin, letting his hand dangle from the "Oh, shit" bar on the door frame. "But my sword—and the switchblade—are consecrated, so it's like jamming a flaming torch against a demon's skin. Rips them right open, lets their essence come spilling out through the hole I make."

Arch looked like he wanted to argue it further, but he didn't. He pulled up in front of the Sinbad Motel and Hendricks hopped out. "I'll be here for a little while, trying to get some answers. Might pop out later, though, for some food."

"Fine," Arch said, and his expression was all unhappiness. "I gotta go run down this drunk when I oughta be trying to figure out how to kill these demons."

Hendricks didn't smile though he wanted to. "The call of duty, huh?" Arch didn't seem to find that funny. Hendricks shut the door and the cop drove off, still looking unhappy.

*

It was an hour or so later that Arch got the call, after finding the black SUV tooling along Gordon Lane at the far end of town. It was a realtor from Knoxville, looking around for properties for one of his clients in Midian, because it was, in her words, "So much more affordable." And only an hour's commute. The commute was too rich for Arch's blood, but then again, he did spend most of his days in the car, so his perspective was probably skewed.

When Arch's phone rang, it took him a minute to realize it wasn't his duty cell; it was his personal one that was going off. He looked at the caller ID and saw Alison's name. She'd talked about personalizing her ring tone but had never got around to it, which was just fine with Arch. He knew that the guys at the station would tease him about it if she did.

"Hey," he said once he'd pushed the button. There was a pause before she started talking.

"Hey, I have to work late tonight," she began.

"Okay," he said but ended up going unheard as she kept talking.

"I'll be home after midnight, and you'd better still be up." She wasn't demanding so much as teasing and coy. Her voice lowered, as though she were afraid someone would overhear. "We've got a baby to make."

"Right," Arch said, not quite sourly but close. Making a baby was almost the last thing on his mind right now. Almost. Practice wasn't unwelcome, but the sole focus on the end result over the process was beginning to irritate him.

"Okay, well, see you later," she said, omitting any one of a dozen cloying nicknames she had for him. "Love you." There wasn't a click, but the call ended, and he put the phone back in the pocket in which he'd been carrying it then frowned. Who knew that making a baby was going to be such a chore? Or come at such an unwelcome time?

It took a few minutes for him to realize he'd only said two words in the whole conversation.

*

Hendricks read his books for about an hour or so. He found it damned hard to concentrate with his stomach growling, though. It didn't take much pondering for him to realize that he really hadn't eaten since yesterday afternoon, unless you counted the beers he'd had last night. Which he didn't. He waited about another fifteen minutes before realizing that really, Arch might not come back for him for quite some time. After all, the big man had been going off-shift when Hendricks had met him at close to midnight last night, which meant he could be hours away from coming back. If he came back. He had looked reasonably pissed at the whole sequence of events before he'd sped away. Hendricks wouldn't have cared for the idea of balancing a job with the profession of demon hunting. Which was why he was thankful he had a patron.

Well, technically a matron, but still. She paid the bills, such as they were.

He stepped outside his hotel room into the sweltering heat at a little after three p.m. and wondered how much longer it was going to be hellishly humid. He guessed quite a while, based on what he'd felt even after the rain last night. Still, and all, the call for food couldn't wait. His stomach was crying out for something. Anything, really.

He was walking along the highway, boots kicking up dust as he scuffed them just to entertain himself, when he sensed a car slowing behind him. He was wearing the drover coat; he had to, in order to hide the sword. It was either that or walk around without it, and that wasn't a palatable option, even if he didn't have some jackass demon named Hollywood interested in wearing his guts for garters. Possibly literally.

Hendricks turned to see a car slowing next to him, a little subcompact. He leaned down to look in the passenger window and saw the blond from the bar, Erin, the one Arch had introduced him to. They just stared at each other for a minute, and he realized he liked the dimples of her cheeks and the way there was just the slightest gap between her teeth when she smiled. Which she was doing right now. "Need a ride somewhere?" she asked, window rolled down.

"I was just about to get something to eat," he answered, unintentionally giving her an "Aw, shucks," grin of his own. It had been called charming, once upon a time. A long time ago.

"Oh, yeah?" She reached across the passenger seat and opened the door for him. "I was going for a late lunch myself, was heading toward the burger joint down the way here." She pointed to a place a few hundred feet away. "If you're interested."

Hendricks didn't really have to think about it; he hopped in, trying not to trip over himself as he did so, and careful to keep the sword wrapped up in the folds of his coat. He wondered how stupid he looked to her, dressed as he was, but he didn't worry too much. She had still stopped, hadn't she? "I'm interested," he said, and kicked himself a second later for making it sound like he was keen for anything other than a burger. He tried to recover. "I was just heading to Fast Freddie's myself, but only because it was the only place I knew."

She giggled, and it was a sweet sound to his ears. "Fast Freddie's is hardly the culinary apex of our town. Come on." She pushed the pedal down and the little car accelerated back onto the road as she checked her mirrors. A pickup blew past only inches away and she swore in a southern twang he found absolutely delightful. "Fucking asshole." He said nothing, waiting to see what she said next. She flushed crimson then jerked her head around, as though she'd forgotten he was there. "Sorry."

Hendricks shrugged, lightly amused. "That's not the sort of thing that puts me off. Having been in the Marines, I've heard a few things that qualify as worse than that."

"I just figured since you were friends with Arch," she said, guiding the car back onto the road a little more calmly, no spray of rubber or gravel as she did so. All told, it was probably the smoothest re-entry to a roadway Hendricks had been involved in, at least since the truck had dropped him off near the overpass only yesterday. "Thought maybe you didn't swear, either." She lowered her voice a little at the last, like she was afraid someone would overhear them.

"Fuck, no," Hendricks said as he shared a grin with her at that. "He really is a serious fellow, though, isn't he?"

"He's a good guy," Erin said, steering the car into the parking lot of a fifties-looking diner. "One of the best, really. You've never met a more decent, churchgoing guy than Arch." She looked over and must have seen the distaste on his face. "What? You got something against someone going to church?"

Hendricks gave it a faint shrug. "Long as they don't go preaching to me, I don't care if someone believes in the flying spaghetti monster, no."

Erin grinned as she pulled the car into the parking space. "Atheist, huh?"

"Among other things." He waited to see if she would do anything other than grin. She didn't. "That doesn't bother you?"

She gave a light shrug of her own, kept smiling. "Doesn't bother me one bit. In fact, I think it's a good thing. It probably means you fuck on the first date." She got out of the car before he could say anything to that. Which was good, because he really didn't have a clue what to say.

*

It was an early day for Arch, clocking out at three in the afternoon. These were normally pretty tough on him, doing a three-to-eleven the night before and turning around to do a seven-to-three today. He felt a bit wired, though. More than a little bit, actually. He knew the demons were weighing on his mind, and all he wanted to do was jab the switchblade that Hendricks had left him through the gut of that Hollywood sonofagun, and twist it good. Justice served. He fingered the hard edge of it in his pocket as he opened the door to the station house, feeling the stale, semi-cool air come back at him.

When he came inside, there was still no one in the waiting area, and no one in sight behind the counter. This was par for the course on a summer afternoon. Erin was probably done for the day; Arch suspected Reeve would pull his wife in to do an unpaid shift because of the budget. The sheriff did these things to keep the station running, but Arch knew he didn't like to. It was the same reason the man ran himself ragged rather than parcel out overtime. Reeve ran the department to the best of his ability, and if something had to suffer, he seemed to think it was his responsibility. Arch had to concede it made him a good boss in a tough spot, though he doubted it won the man many points with the voters who elected him. It's not like they knew.

Reeve poked his head out of his office, looking toward the front desk. "Oh, good, it's you."

"Just me," Arch said as he rounded the front counter. "Here to clock out."

"Hey," Reeve said, like he'd just remembered something. "You ever get around to MacGruder's place?"

Arch had been dreading this question all day. Not so much for his answer, which he'd already planned out, but for the follow-up questions that might come after. "I did. And you're not gonna believe what I found out there."

"Oh, really?" Reeve waited a second, like Arch would go on without prompting.

He did. "Yeah. Kellen, Munson, that whole bunch. Said MacGruder hired them as hands while he was away."

Reeve didn't scoff but damned close. "Those idiots?"

"I know," Arch said. "But the place looked clean, and it's not like MacGruder was around to back them up. They said he was away for a few days."

Reeve treaded the line between skepticism and an *Are-you-an-idiot?* look. "You didn't catch a whiff of anything else? Like them lying or hiding the MacGruders under the floorboards or anything?"

"Didn't see nothing like that," Arch said, reminding himself that if Reeve got a bug up his ass and decided to check out the farm for himself, he would almost certainly be killed. "Said they'd be back in a few days, you could check with them then." On the other hand, when MacGruder never showed up again, Arch didn't want to have to lie more than necessary. Pinning the blame on Munson's crew was honest—though in a roundabout sort of way. Buried in the lies. He didn't let that bubble up on him right now, though, because there'd be plenty of time for the guilt about it after he'd tidied up the demons. However that was gonna happen.

"All right," Reeve said, but his face was a mask of dark clouds. "Those boys are low-grade pains in the ass, but I don't see them making the leap to murder and home invasion and then lying about it." His hand came down to scratch his chin. "Yeah, maybe. I mean, Old MacGruder's given second chances to worse workers than those four deadbeats." He smiled, a thin, wry one. "Hell, I'm gonna have me a laugh later, just trying to imagine those four at the back end of a cow trying to get milk out. MacGruder will be lucky if the whole herd don't have mastitis by the time he gets back." He gave it a moment's more thought and his face turned serious. "It'd be nice if those shitheads got their acts straight. I could stand to go without arresting them anymore."

"Agreed," Arch said, turning back toward the time clock. Reeve gave him a vague wave as he finished up and sat down to do his after-shift report. He hoped setting the lies he'd just told down on paper would help him remember them better.

*

"See, I learned this lesson from … Clooney, I think it was," Hollywood was saying from the back seat, talking to Sleeveless as they cruised along the highway into town. "He was talking about how you always have to get back to being in the character's head, how it always comes back to motivation."

"You know Clooney?" Sleeveless said from the front seat, turning his head a little so he could look back at Hollywood.

"Sure, sure," Hollywood said. It was true, sort of. He'd shaken the man's hand once or twice at parties. The lesson was from an episode of *Inside the Actor's Studio*, though. "Anyway, always going back to a character's motivation." Hollywood stared straight ahead. It was late afternoon, the sky was still blue, which was disconcerting for their type, though not painful. Like he imagined it was for humans who were awake all night; some were better suited to it than others. "So, I'm looking at these two characters we're dealing with, and I'm wondering … what's their motivation?"

Sleeveless didn't answer at first, obedient, probably making sure he didn't trip over his boss, pausing before continuing. Good. Very good. Finally, he said, "Well, the cop is just a pain in the ass—"

"The cop," Hollywood cut Sleeveless off, "may be a pain in the ass, but he's operating outside the purview of a normal cop. Cops don't work with demon hunters." He settled back in his seat and fingered one of the numerous holes in his shirt. He'd shed the coat after it had been ruined. The shirt was in marginally better shape. Still ruined, but probably not noticeably in this shit town. "So you guys go and give away that you're demons, he runs, and he gets a demon hunter. These are not normal actions for the police, who don't know the first fucking thing about our world." He concentrated. "But then, once we get past that hurdle, we arrive at the idea—okay, he knows what a demon is, he knows a demon hunter, he runs and gets said demon hunter after being confronted with demons. That makes logical sense."

Sleeveless waited through another moment of silence. "So … why would anyone become a demon hunter?"

Hollywood smiled. "That's a good question, and goes right to the heart of motivation. Because it's not like it's lucrative. I mean, even a lesser's cash tends to get sucked up in the vortex when they get pulled back to the nethers. And they're almost all bums anyway." He watched Sleeveless tense up. "You know what I mean. Very little money, working shit jobs, maybe—maybe—slicing off a human for a special treat every now and again, but mostly living under the radar so they can keep their heads down. Even the ones that thrive on hotspots, moving around, preying on humans when the dinner bell rings, they don't tend to keep much in the way of human money. Bad long-term planners, except for a few."

"Of course there's the fundamentalists," Hollywood went on. "I met a so-called human supremacist one time." Sleeveless let out a chuckle as Hollywood went on. "Can you believe that shit? Like humans are supreme at anything other than wearing skin better than we do." He flicked his wrist, waving his hand away. "You get the crusaders every once in a while, though, the ones who do it for religious reasons. 'Demons bad!' and all that shit. Which …" he had to concede, "we sort of are, it's just there's some of us better at it than others."

"What about the ones that do it for the rush?" Sleeveless said. "I met one of those a long time ago, outside Detroit."

"A thrill-killer?" Hollywood said, nodding. "Yeah, I've run across a couple. Think they're hot shit, looking for a way to kill without going to jail." He smiled. "I guess not leaving a body behind is one way to go about it. But I don't think that's this guy. Maybe, but … I dunno, there's something else there. Doubtful it's religion, or that he's a supremacist." The supremacist hadn't even talked to him, told him anything, until he'd started peeling the man's flesh off. Then he'd started spilling his guts. Literally. "Thrill-killers are egomaniacs sometimes. Like to keep trophies if they can, cut off an ear before they finish the job. They know about essence, how it spills out, and lots of times they try to capture it, bottle it for sale." He thought back to last night. "Those boys were covered in it, like they hadn't even bothered to catch it." He thought about it again, saw the look on the smaller one's face, the white boy, as he was straining against the minion's arm. "No, I think I've got them figured."

"Oh, yeah?" Sleeveless asked. "How's that?"

"The cop was looking for the farmer," Hollywood said, pensive, as the car rattled down the road. "He's a law and order type, trying to figure out how to adapt to the situation at hand. Simple guy. Doing his best, given what he's got to work with. But the demon hunter, he's something else. He's not into any of those things we just went through. He's doing this for his own reasons." He'd seen the guy's face as he'd tipped the hat off and gone for the knife. It wasn't just scrunched with exertion. "Something personal." It was laced with anger, and not just a fury at being restrained, either.

"Oh?" Sleeveless asked. "What, did Kellen insult his mother or something?"

Hollywood chuckled. "No, not that. Not him. No, what we've got here is a stone demon killer. Cold heart. Black. Not in it for money, ego, or fun, not religion, nor supremacy." He didn't let it get to him, but if he was a chickenshit like Sleeveless, he might have felt a little chill thinking about what this guy was, what was behind him. What he might be willing to do, because of his reason for being here. "No … this guy … he's here for revenge."

Chapter 7

Arch had dropped by Hendricks's motel room, knocked on the door, and gotten no response. He was tempted to ask the manager of the Sinbad for a key. He'd talked to him earlier, could see the recognition in the man's eyes. He was clearly a fan of Arch's from back in the day. Arch still got that and mostly didn't mind. It tended to produce cooperation of a kind not necessarily enjoyed by other members of the department. In some cases, that counted for more than others. He considered himself lucky when all it did was make them think of him as a man asking for help rather than a cop trying to get them to give something up.

He didn't push it, though, not yet. Odds were that Hendricks was elsewhere, maybe getting a bite, and he was all set to drive by a couple of the restaurants when his phone went off again. He picked it up, saw it was Alison, and answered. "Hey, babe."

"Hey," she came back. "You're off now, right?"

"Just clocked out a few minutes ago," he said, answering automatically. "Why?"

"Meet me at the apartment?" Her voice was hopeful, honey laced with extra sugar. Not enough to gag him, just enough to recognize it for what it was. "I got a break, figured instead of getting some supper, we'd just … satisfy some other cravings."

Arch wasn't far gone enough on working this demon thing that he was unresponsive, but it did produce a little resistance in him. He shut it up pretty quick by remembering that Hendricks was indisposed in some way right now, anyhow. "Sure. I can drop by home for a little bit. You got a half hour off?"

"Yep," she said, "and I'm leaving now."

"Okay," he said, "you'll beat me home by about five minutes, probably."

"Hurry, hurry," she teased. "See you then."

Once he'd hung up, he took one last look at the door to Hendricks's room. The demons could wait a half hour or so. Besides, he needed to eat anyway.

*

"So now we know what our players are up to," Hollywood said as they rounded the corner of road that was semi-paved. "The next question is, who are they?"

"Krauther's on the cowboy," Sleeveless said, pulling off the road onto a gravel driveway. "Seems like he's new in town. But I know the cop. We've had dealings before."

"I figured that out," Hollywood said. He was sure Sleeveless missed the irony he had laced the statement with. He wasn't bright enough to understand concepts like that.

"His name's Archibald Stan," Sleeveless went on. "Was a local football hero, graduated and went to UT in Knoxville. Married the head cheerleader—"

"They still married?" Hollywood asked with obvious interest. He felt himself leaning forward in his seat and everything.

"Yeah," Sleeveless said. "She works down at Rogerson's, the grocery store in town. Her daddy bought it out from the widow Rogerson after her husband died."

"Good, good," Hollywood said, putting all his thoughts into a matrix. "So he's got vulnerabilities. His little cheerleader wife." He felt his nose twist. "Not that it really matters. If he's too problematic of a sacrifice, there are plenty of others. Though I do want to make him hurt for what he did to my suit."

"Your suit?" There was an air of disbelief from Sleeveless, like something he'd said was unfathomable.

"This suit cost more than your whole town," Hollywood replied, burying his irritation. He gave the feeling a moment to subside. "So … Krauther is on the cowboy now?"

"Says he's staying at the motel," Sleeveless said, "right near where we saw them last night."

"And these guys you know," Hollywood said, gesturing to the trailer that was peeking out from between the trees ahead, just a little farther up the gravel path, "they'll be okay with … getting done what needs to get done?"

"Yeah," Sleeveless said. "They're pretty hard. They've killed people before, I know it. If they know you're backing us," Sleeveless turned a little red, "and paying, then they'll be willing to get out of line to get the job done."

Hollywood waited just a second. "And they're not as stupid as the last two?"

Sleeveless hesitated before answering. "Well, they're not as smart as me."

Hollywood sighed. It was so hard to find good help in this shithole town.

*

"So where are you from?" Erin asked with that drawl. He was loving the drawl, the southern accent.

"Amery, Wisconsin," Hendricks replied, taking a sip of his pop. He called it pop, she'd said Coke, even though the Pepsi signs were clearly posted. He just kind of shook his head at that. "You probably never heard of it. It's small."

"Oh?" She looked like she was interested. At least more interested in him than she was in what was left of her meal, which wasn't much. She'd gone through the big burger in no time, and was picking at the last few fries, which looked like they'd gone cold, all mushy and limp. "Like … smaller than Midian?"

He looked out the window. "Maybe a little. We didn't have a Wal-Mart, that was for sure, you had to go to St. Croix Falls or New Richmond for one of those." He paused, realizing those names were meaningless to her. "You had to drive a little ways. Twenty minutes, maybe."

"Sounds familiar," she said then explained. "The Wal-Mart's new. Only opened in my junior year of high school."

"When was that?" he asked, more than a little curious. She looked young. Younger than him.

"Ummm," she said, a little grin on her face, shy. "Two years ago, I think." She met his gaze, fed off it. "I'm nineteen."

On a purely intellectual level, Hendricks didn't know what to think about that. He was dimly aware that he wasn't really going on intellect, not around her. "It's a good age. I remember being that young, vaguely."

"How old are you now?" She said it all flirty, like there was a giggle just waiting to escape.

"Twenty-five," he said, matter-of-fact.

"An older man." She didn't make it sound like a bad thing. "So how do you know Arch?"

"Oh, we go way back," Hendricks said. Lying was no great stretch for him, though he didn't like it. The alternative was trying to explain how he was a demon hunter that had met the man only last night. It was an answer designed to keep Arch from looking like an idiot and him in the running for that first-date fuck she'd alluded to. If he were honest with himself, though, Arch's reputation didn't fit very large into that equation. "How'd you know him?"

"Everybody 'round here knows Arch," she said, nibbling on a soggy fry. "Hard not to. I didn't really know him very well until we started working together at the Sheriff's Department, though, on account of he was three years ahead of me in school. I knew his wife some, though, she was cheerleading captain when I was a freshman."

"You were a cheerleader?" He watched her blush. "I could see that."

"Only for a year," she said, still red in the cheeks. He thought it was damned cute. "It was too much for me."

"Hey," he said, a thought occurring to him. "If you're only nineteen, how were you drinking in the bar last night?"

"Oh, that?" she waved a hand across the table at him, close enough he was tempted to reach out and catch it, hold her hand. "Please. Sheriff's Department budget is so strained, Reeve doesn't waste his time with stuff like that. Fast Freddie's serves minors all the time. But," she held up a finger to wag at him, "Phil, the barman, won't let you drive if you're underage. Makes you give your keys to him before he'll pour, so you gotta get another ride home if you're drinking."

Hendricks smiled at that thought. "So you're a sheriff's deputy, blatantly flouting the law, huh?"

"There's a lot of laws I flout. Did you know under Tennessee law, it's still technically illegal for me to give you a blow job?" She took a sip of her drink, but kept her eyes on him.

For the second time, Hendricks was flummoxed. This time he just tried not to look dumb while he recovered, trying to keep his mouth shut instead of agape. After a moment, he said, "Well, I've always thought if you were gonna break a law, you oughta at least make it one you'll enjoy breaking."

*

It wasn't a traditional job interview. Hollywood had done those, hiring crew, even been involved in casting decisions, table reads, shit like that. This wasn't like any of those. This was sitting around a trailer that smelled of weed and loserhood, not in equal measure. There was way more loserhood than weed in the air, and that was saying something.

The boys lined up in front of him on the couch looked like they were feral, wild demons of a type he didn't even really know, not off the top of his head. Little things, really, common as fucking dirt on earth. It would have been too much to ask for a greater to be mixed in with this handful of meth-heads. Greaters didn't drift around waiting to be henchmen for other greaters. They didn't lack purpose like these disposable louts, who worked in petty human jobs until something came around for them. Greaters did shit with their lives. Seized moments. Cut a path to success through the brambly bushes of adversity.

Hollywood sniffed the air. Also, almost all of the greaters showered regularly. Which clearly hadn't happened here.

They mostly wore t-shirts and shorts, and really, they all kind of looked the same to Hollywood. Which probably meant all was right in the world. If one of them wanted to distinguish himself (or herself, he noted with some surprise, because there was a female in there with them, though it was hard to tell given the hairy legs) they'd clean up, start wearing something more presentable. He doubted any of them would do that, though.

"So," Hollywood said, letting it ooze out and trying to create the right impression from the start. He was seated in a battered old chair that stank like someone had let a dog lay in it every night. There were no dogs in the trailer. None. "I trust …" he struggled to remember Sleeveless's name, the one he'd given, and gave up after only a moment's effort, instead gesturing toward the man in the flannel with the cut-off sleeves, "our mutual … friend …" he struggled with that word, "has informed you that I'm looking for some muscle to help me finish the job I've got going in this town?" He waited for the nods, which came, some slower than others. He'd hoped the woman would nod first, but she was somewhere in the middle. He looked over the sea of white faces, and then turned to Sleeveless. "Do we not have any … diversity candidates?"

Sleeveless just stared back at him blankly. "They're all demons …?"

Hollywood smiled faintly, realizing once again he was talking to an idiot. "I mean … do we not have any that might be more representative of other racial backgrounds?" He gave a patronizing smile. "I realize we have a female in our midst, and that's good, but I just meant some more ethnic diversity. More breadth."

Sleeveless gave him a cockeyed look. "You know their skin ain't really real, right? It's just a shell—"

"I fucking know that, you idiot," Hollywood said sharply. "I'm just asking if we can add in some muscle that maybe has a little different shade on their shell, so we don't look so fucking monochromatic. Do you not know any African-Americans or Hispanic-Americans—hell, or Asian-Americans we could add to the pool?"

Sleeveless was rendered speechless by this, sputtering. "You asked for demons, I brought you to the only demons I know …"

Hollywood sighed, feeling a throbbing in his head caused by his essence bulging in his shell. He could feel things through the skin, of course, probably just like a human could, and right now he felt his true self wanting to escape, burst out and rip the head off Sleeveless for being a dumb fuck. He'd given it some thought, wondering how humans felt, back when he was considering being an actor, and after a long time he'd concluded that humans couldn't possibly feel things the way his kind could. Demon essences reached beyond the shell, could taste, touch, smell and feel things that brushed up against them. Not just the physical, but the metaphysical as well. Which was just another reason humans were a low form of life, just above ferrets.

"Okay, all right, yeah," Hollywood said at last. It really wasn't all right, of course. "We'll just have to make do with a lily-white cast for now and keep our eyes open for other candidates to balance things out as we go." It probably didn't matter that much longer anyway, but it burned him; he was in charge of this—production, for lack of a better word, and the way things were just looked … unseemly, to his way of thinking. He divided the couch in half. "You three, go meet up with Krauther," (what a dumb name) "at the cowboy's motel." He thought about it for a second. "Wait, you know what you're supposed to be doing, right?" He shook his head. "Never mind, that's too much to ask. You know Krauther?" He waited, and the nods came again. "Go find him at that fleabag motel by the interstate, and he'll tell you what to do."

One of them stood up abruptly, and Hollywood smiled. "Good. Someone's got initiative." He waved at the other two. "Go on." He reached in his pocket and pulled out a wad of bills. "Here." Threw a Franklin at each of them. "For your day's labor." They filed out, and he turned to look at the four who were left. "You guys are gonna get marching orders from Sleeveless." He smiled. "We have something planned for one of your local cops, something special."

It was the woman who smiled first. He liked that. Predator's instinct. "You're gonna run this team," he said to her then waved at Sleeveless. "He'll tell you what to do." He peeled off four hundred-dollar bills and handed one to each of them, careful not to touch their hands, then found his way out the door, pushing the old screen door on the outside of the trailer out of the way as he stepped down. The flies weren't as thick here as at the dairy farm, but they were still present. Still annoying. But at least out here he could breathe.

*

Alison was already inside when Arch got home, the sound of soft footsteps coming toward him on the thin carpeting of their apartment. He put his keys in their familiar spot on the table next to the door then relieved himself of his cell phones, both of them. By that time he heard her near the end of the hall, coming out of the bedroom. He caught a glimpse out of the corner of his eye, a little splash of red, and he turned his head to see.

She was leaned against the frame of the bedroom door like a pinup model, arching her back, bare feet on the carpet, showing off her long legs, tan from the long hours she spent out on the balcony of the apartment and beside her momma and daddy's pool. His eyes followed them all the way up to the red piece of lingerie she was wearing, something that reminded him just a little of a one-piece bathing suit but pared back considerably. All the important pieces were covered, bikini-like. A see-through lace panel, which hung loosely from the bra, delicately covered her trim waistline.

Arch wasn't quite sure what to make of the whole ensemble nor did he really want to give it too much thought. Any thoughts of demons slipped out of his mind as he looked at her, standing there in the faded afternoon light that seeped into the apartment through the closed curtains. This was hardly the first time she'd done this, dressed up for him in this way. It was one of her favorite things, judging by the bills from Victoria's Secret, which was one reason why he didn't complain. She'd done it more since they'd decided to try for a baby, but it was hardly a new occurrence before that. And it wasn't for nothing, either; there was a very simple reason why she kept doing it.

Because it worked every time.

He crossed toward where she waited, giving him a very forward look, using her index finger to beckon him onward with a slow, sexy, come-hither motion. And a few minutes later, after she had gone first, he did indeed come. Hither and yon.

*

She'd wanted to get a beer, and Hendricks had gone along with it. Who was he to argue with what the lady wanted, after all? They'd debated walking to Fast Freddie's from the burger joint and ultimately decided against it. Too damned hot, they'd both concluded before hopping into her little subcompact. It wasn't much cooler in there, Hendricks reflected as they drove the hundred yards or so to the bar's parking lot before getting out. The car's air conditioning hadn't even had a chance to start working before they were done with the drive.

The light dimmed as he walked into the bar. It was a little like a cave, dark and unpleasant. There was still smoke in the air, unlike lots of the bars he went to nowadays in cities. Anti-smoking ordinances had forced the cigarettes outside to the parking lot. Hendricks was mostly indifferent on that score; he didn't mind being around smoke and sometimes even preferred it when he was drinking. Sometimes he'd buy a pack when he was wasted, just chain-smoke his way through it, barely inhaling. It felt good, having a beer in one hand, cigarette in the other. When he was sober, he couldn't even stand the smell of them.

Erin walked in front of him, striding up to the bar before slapping her keys down and giving him a sidelong look. "Now, if I'm gonna drink here, I can't drive home, so I'll need some place to sleep it off later." She was straight-faced this time, probing him for a response.

He tried to decide whether to open up and be as blatant as she had been but decided that subtle was probably better from him; women could get away with bold and make it sexy. "I might know a place within stumbling distance." He smiled a little when he said it and hoped it was just right.

She got impish. "Oh, do you?" She slid the keys toward the barman, who wordlessly picked them up and made them disappear under the bar. "Well, all right then. Set us up, Phil."

The barman nodded and a couple glasses were filled and on the bar a moment later. She led Hendricks toward a corner of the bar under a Miller sign and when he sat down at a table, she dragged her chair over to sit almost on top of him. That was fine by him, because she smelled just the faintest bit of sweat but mostly of a fragrance that was girly and sweet, something he had caught only in passing before. She was right there next to him, close enough to lean into, close enough to touch, her beer sweating on the table just beside his.

"So," she said, breathing at him, her perfume mixing with the faint hint of beer on her breath, as she shuffled to untuck her buttoned-up khaki uniform top from her pants. It looked a little sloppy, totally at odds with what he'd come to expect from her, but he was still pretty damned smitten. "What should we talk about?"

He gave it a second's thought as he took a pull of his beer. "The weather is the normal topic in ice breaker situations like this, I think."

"It's fucking hot, without the fucking. At least at the moment." He didn't miss the suggestion as she took another drink, putting her glass back down half-empty. "You've got some catching up to do." He took her meaning and drained the rest in one long gulp. She blinked, a little impressed. He set it back on the table and she held up two fingers to Phil, who nodded from his lonely place behind the bar, only one other customer in the entire establishment. "So," she said again, "what should we talk about?"

He felt the first gentle stirrings of a buzz, just barely. "I don't really know. I'm not much of a conversationalist anymore, honestly. Out of practice, I suppose."

"Hm." She sort of frowned, twisting her lips by puckering them to one side and then the other before looking back up at him. "We could just make out."

He thought about asking her if that would be out of place in a joint like Fast Freddie's, but the thought fell by the wayside as she leaned in and put her lips on his with just the right amount of pressure, the smell of the beer on her breath a kind of sweet, heady perfume all its own as his tongue found hers.

*

Arch was lying on his back, breathing heavily, his head leaning against the bed near the headboard. His pillow had gotten knocked off some time during their romp, he wasn't sure exactly when. It wasn't a pressing concern, not at the moment. He'd entered the dreamy, sleepy state of post-coitus where very little mattered. Two days of long shifts, short sleep and bizarre events had drained him, and it was showing. A few things were prickling at the back of his mind, things he knew he needed to do, but they was so far back in the haze of tired that he couldn't quite grasp them.

"I have to go," Alison muttered into his bicep. He opened his eyes enough to look down at where she lay rested against his side, her pale skin against his dark, blond hair spilling over his arm like a waterfall of yellow. She sat up, bare to him, and somewhere south he felt a stir, like he could maybe go again in a little while. Not yet, though. He was still settled into a nice fog of afterglow.

"Go where?" he murmured, not really thinking it over.

"Back to work." She rolled to the edge of the bed, letting her legs hang over as she sat up, her bare back facing him. His eyes crawled over it, noting for the millionth time the lack of tan lines. It provided a nice aesthetic continuity. He wanted to reach out and stroke her starting from the shoulder on down to the top of her crack, but he couldn't quite find the energy for it at the moment. Maybe later.

He let his eyes drift shut again, and though he was dimly aware of the sounds of her moving about the room, fetching clothes from the floor, it only came to him in drifts, followed by what felt like long periods of missing time. He felt her kiss and it stirred him enough to open his eyes again. She was sitting on the bed next to him now, looking down with a sweet smile. “Hey,” he said quietly, still sleepy.

“I love you,” she said, and kissed him, leaning over, the soft cotton of her polo shirt pushed against his chest.

“Love you, too, babe,” he said, and let his eyes drift shut.

“I’ll be back late,” she said, words drifting into his consciousness from somewhere above.

“Mmhmm.” He was drifting off again, dimly aware that her footsteps were receding now. The smell of her perfume—a trendy one from a department store she visited down in Chattanooga—was still hanging in the air, along with the earthier smell of his sweat. His muscles were at peace, worn out, relaxed. He rolled his head sideways and the scent of the laundry detergent from the sheets wafted up at him, something just a little fruity, like apple. They felt soft, and he was perfectly content to lie like this, just like this, maybe for the rest of the night. He heard her in the kitchen, grabbing a bottle of water out of the fridge before leaving, like she always did.

The next sound he heard was the front door crashing in, wood breaking off its hinges, and the sound of Alison’s screams vaulted him back to immediate consciousness.

Chapter 8

Hendricks remembered he liked making out. He hadn't done a ton of it in high school but enough to get by. It was the frustrating kind of making out back then, though, the kind that didn't ever last long enough, the kind that didn't hold the promise of sweeter things to come, the crescendo at the end of all that buildup. Second base, maybe, if he'd been lucky. He hadn't gotten laid until the summer after high school ended, just about on his way out of town headed to Basic. It had been awkward and unexpected, without any making out to start things off, which put it at odds with his whole high school experience. All finish, no buildup. Which might have been part of the reason it was so awkward.

Erin's tongue probed his, and the collective taste of their beers was heavy. They'd been at the bar for something like an hour, kissing almost the whole time. They were taking frequent breaks for hydration, though (not really, not unless beer hydrated; in Hendricks's experience, it did just the opposite), during which they exchanged long, meaningful stares as they sipped their beers quietly, without saying anything.

This time, after they broke apart to take a breath, Erin finally said something. "Aren't you going to invite me back to your motel room?" There was a hint of impatience there, as she downed the rest of her mug. It was her fourth.

"Yep," Hendricks said, nodding, finishing his beer as she stood, her fingers finding his, holding his hand and helping to pull him to his feet as the last of the cold beer sluiced down his throat.

*

Arch was a little slow stumbling out of bed, the deep drifting feeling despoiled by the sudden screams and sounds of his door being broken into pieces, torn from its hinges as he scrambled for his pants, which he was pretty sure were somewhere between the bed he was on and the door that was being busted apart. His eyes found them a little outside the bedroom, and he stumbled to his knees. Alison was just a little in front of him, her hand over her mouth, screaming. There were hands reaching through the top half of the solid door, which was broken cleanly at the middle, and being pushed to the side. With one last screech and crack it gave and the door came open in pieces, just as he pulled his gun with his right hand and dug the switchblade Hendricks had lent him out of his pants pocket and let it flip open with his left.

*

She tasted good, like he remembered a woman should taste, all warm on his lips. Even the heat out in the parking lot wasn't bothering him. They'd paused on the blacktop, hands all over each other, fumbling a little each time they stopped. Then they'd walk a spell further, hand in hand, little shared glances full of significant meaning. The significance to Hendricks was that it looked like she'd be tearing his clothes off the minute they got back to the motel. He worried only a little about that, planning to ball up the drover coat and get it off first and foremost, along with his belt, which he would have to unfasten first. If he did it right, he could get the sword off and keep it from clattering by taking the coat off properly. The gun would be only a little more complicated; if he kept his body aligned just so while they were undressing, odds were she'd never even notice it as he stepped out of his jeans. Besides, her eyes were closed every time they were kissing. He'd checked.

They paused to kiss on the overpass, dusk just starting to settle. Hendricks let his mind wander a little this time, as he put a hand at the small of her back and crept it up her uniform top. Seemed like it was getting close to seven in the evening or so. He was pretty damned buzzed, but she was absolutely hammered. He stopped his hand at the clasp of her bra, just making sure he knew where it was, getting a general feel for it. For later.

They started walking again, and he let her get out in front of him just a bit and watched her ass. It was good, very good, wriggling with each step in her khakis, the faint traces of her underwear visible. The top of her undies was visible, too, because he hadn't fully removed his hand from her back yet, keeping her shirt just a little up. The small of her back had a little tattoo, something circular with spikes, like an artist's rendition of a sunrise. He couldn't see it very well now, but he had a feeling he'd get a better look at it real soon. Maybe for an extended period of time, if he had his way.

*

Arch waited for the arms breaking through his door to be followed by bodies, things he could shoot at. He'd refilled the magazine in his Glock twice in the last twenty-four hours, and it looked like soon he'd need to do it a third time. He stood and got Alison by the shoulder, pushing her back behind him. Her fingers clutched at his arm, nails digging into his flesh in purest fear. He felt her press into him, her cloth pants against his right butt cheek, and he remembered that he was naked, and spared only a thought to wondering if that made him vulnerable before aiming down the sights of his pistol and firing the first round as a head popped through the door.

*

The parking lot of the motel was packed red clay, and with the sun going down the whole scene looked a little like what he remembered Florida to be like. Dusty, kind of orange-ish, like some sort of cross between Italian villas and tropical paradise. The Sinbad was neither of those things, but it was dusty, and orange in the sunset. Erin stumbled along beside him, having a little more trouble walking than he was. Not that he was having an easy time of it, just easier than her. Keeping up with her on beers had been a bad idea.

She swayed, and he let her walk out in front of him again, put his hand on her ass while letting a big grin slip out on his face. It had been a long time. Without the alcohol, he might even have found a way to talk himself out of it. He'd done that a couple times before, once in a town in Montenegro, and another time just outside New Orleans. That one had been easy—or harder, depending on how you looked at it.

That wasn't going to happen this time, though. He could feel the stiffness in his jeans. He'd been ready for an hour or more. She stopped and kissed him again, just outside the door to his room, and he unbuckled her belt then slid a hand down the front of her pants, teasing. His fingers went further south then got really slick, and he figured out that she was apparently ready, too.

*

Arch shot twice, a double tap at the first face to reveal itself through the door. It looked human when he first saw it, but the gunshots broke that facade away quickly, revealing something else; a face twisted around the edges and distorted, the eyes, nose and mouth lit by something that looked like fire bleeding out from within. The body that it was attached to staggered then was pushed aside by another man. This one Arch knew, a guy who'd been picked up by Reeve for possession a couple times, a real meth-head, though he showed none of the obvious scarring. Arch put two rounds in his face and the guy stalled in his advance.

*

Hendricks fumbled for his key. The motel had one of the old-fashioned locks, and he was going at it left handed and blind, since his right hand was presently occupied down Erin's pants and she had her hands on his face as she kissed him, moaning a little as he swayed with her, listening to the key scrape against the door, then hit the frame as he tried to find the lock without looking at it. It might take a while, but he was happy enough doing what he was doing that he was okay with that.

He opened his eyes when he heard footsteps over Erin's moans, the sound of urgency, of feet running. He looked up just in time to see someone hit Erin with a solid push from the side. She stumbled, already a little unbalanced, and her head hit the door frame to his left. She fell soundlessly, her moaning cut off with a final, "Ohhh—"

Hendricks backed against the door, dropping the key and found himself outnumbered, four to one. They rushed him before he could recover enough presence of mind to get a hand on his sword.

*

"Get in the bedroom and lock the door!" Arch shouted as he shrugged out of Alison's tight grasp, breaking her grip on his arm. He advanced on the first of the demons, the meth head, and shot him again in the face, causing the man to stagger back. Arch jumped forward and hit him in the chest with the switchblade, tugging it down like he was ripping a hole in a piece of canvas. It took some strength, but Arch had that. Maybe even more right now because he was fighting naked, his wife—his whole world—just behind him. He was the only thing standing between her and these things.

*

Hendricks should have been dead, going hand to hand with four demons. He should have been ripped apart in the first five seconds of the fight. He hadn't died though, he'd shoulder-charged the nearest of them and hit him in a football tackle that would have probably drawn criticism from someone who'd actually played the sport, like Arch. But it put the guy down and that was what mattered, right?

They were fast and he was drunk. He spared a look to make sure Erin was all right, and she was, as near as he could tell. A thin line of blood was running down her scalp from the side of her head, but it looked like it was all. She was slumped against his door, just looking like she'd had too much to drink and hadn't quite made it inside before passing out.

He didn't have time to think about it, though, because the other three were coming at him. He'd learned to fight multiple opponents at a time in the Marines, in martial arts training. It was all predicated on keeping the fight to one-on-one at all times. With humans, that wasn't too hard. You just had to be highly mobile and good with a kick, keeping them at bay until you could score some points—or put them down, hard, in a real fight. Hendricks was good with a kick under normal conditions. Right now he didn't trust himself too much with one, for fear he'd fall down by aiming at the wrong guy. His reflexes were for shit, absolutely destroyed by the booze. If he lived, he'd take himself to task for being such a dumbass as to take his eye off the ball in order to soothe his balls. He could have at least maybe waited until the demon thing that he'd already set to simmering was taken care of before trying to take advantage of his opportunity with Erin, but clearly it had just been too long since he'd gotten laid, because he wasn't thinking with the right head.

As drunk as he was, the demons had to have been enjoying a high of their own because they were moving slower than any demons he'd ever grappled with before. For a moment, he questioned whether they were in fact demons at all, but he landed a hard, wobbling cross on the jaw of one of them and saw two things. One, the guy ignored the pain, and two, the eyes—the windows to the man's soul—flared with fire, genuine and real. Demon essence to the core. Hendricks gave him a hard, drunken shove that was surprisingly effective and the man lost his footing and tumbled onto his back.

Hendricks wanted to feel triumphant about it, but the one he'd already tackled was back on his feet, so it was still three on one. He circled left to put one of them between him and the other two, and tried to figure out his next move.

*

Arch fired again, but now there were three of them, and they were all in his apartment. Two guys and one girl, all mug shots he recognized, all multi-time losers that he knew were stronger than he was and also more clothed. The clothed part still bothered him, which he found a little funny at a moment he was fighting for his life.

Two of them came at him at once while the other writhed on the floor from catching a slug in the face, and he fired twice at the one on the left, delaying him. He changed targets to the woman, then realized his action was open, the last bullet fired. If she hadn't been practically on top of him, he would have tried a combat reload. As it was, he committed the cardinal sin in a fight: he hesitated.

She slammed into him with all the fury of someone high enough to feel no pain from the impact. Arch felt himself get whipped through the air and onto the ground, landing hard on his back. He managed to roll enough so that he didn't get the wind knocked out of him, but he was still down, and a demon woman who was stronger than him was on top of him. He felt her fist hit him in the chest, right on the sternum. The second hit him in the ribs, causing him to fold in pain.

*

Hendricks found himself four on one again, despite his best efforts. The only bright spot for him was that he was being enough of a pain in the ass to them that not one of them had gone for Erin yet. Which was fortunate, because if they had any brains, they would have played her as the hostage long ago and probably wrapped things up by now.

They were smart enough to keep bunched up on him, though, and it was keeping him from even getting a chance to pull his sword. Five times he'd had his hand on the hilt, raising it up, and they'd slammed into him, or forced him to roll, not giving him the distance to draw it out. He was about to get frustrated, and was ready to do something he knew he shouldn't. Screw it, though, as slow as these bastards were, it was still life or death. He had his hand on the grip of his pistol and was about to pull it to fire from the hip when one of them got a hand on him.

*

Arch hadn't been hit—really hit—since his last year of college football. He'd worn pads for that, though, and in this case there was literally nothing between the crack of demon fist and his body, skin and muscle, and bone. He didn't feel anything break, but it damned sure hurt, and he didn't care for that, nossir. He bucked, arching his back and pushing the demon off him enough to get the switchblade around. He slashed across her face as she dodged back, toppling off him and letting him do no more than slice her across the cheek.

He started to roll to his feet but another of them slammed into his side. This one was the one he'd stalled at the door, recovered from the gunshots to the face. Arch grimaced from the impact and hit the floor again.

*

Hendricks was in the grip of one of them, taking a hit to the jaw for his stupidity in not pulling the gun earlier. That was dumb. If he couldn't pull his sword, why not at least get a hand on the gun? It could have bought him a few seconds, maybe, and that might have been just enough. But no, he had been too concerned with the attention it would draw, playing careful to avoid the law, when he really should have been playing careful the other way. The way that avoided death.

He got hit again, and he couldn't decide whether the alcohol was helping him take the punches better by muting the pain or dulling his senses so that every hit took longer to recover from. He didn't come to a conclusion on that, mostly because of the sudden, searing agony he felt in the region of his chest as the one that had him slapped a hand against his shirt, wrestler-style.

If a normal guy had done it, it might have stung. When the demon did it, it shredded the fabric and left him with thin lines at the points of each finger impact, like Hendricks had just been whipped there. The demon was a malevolent son of a bitch, he could see that through his pained, drunken haze. There was a big grin looking him right in the face. The slap came down again, harder this time, and Hendricks felt the blood run down his chest under his shirt.

*

Arch hit the ground again, and his head ran into the wall. He was pushed tight against the wall, his face mashed against the dull white paint, the color Alison had been begging him to paint over since they moved in. His hands were empty, he dimly realized, now unsure of where the switchblade was. The demon had an arm against his neck, and all the thing's weight was on him, holding him down, as he looked into the kitchen, toward where the demon woman had rolled after he forced her off of him.

There was a smell of powder from where he'd splintered the drywall hanging in his nose, and he felt blood coming down, too, settling on his lips with a distinctive metallic taste. He could hear his own breathing, the pounding of his heart. His right eye was mashed against the wall so he couldn't even see straight. The aches and pains were all there, along with the sense of the elbow of the creature that was on him, ready to break his spine. That was all bad. Very, very bad. But it was nothing compared to what he saw in front of him.

Standing in the kitchen, the female demon had her hands out, wrapped around a soft—very soft, as he remembered from just a few minutes earlier—target. She had her tongue out of her mouth, hands wrapped around a body, one hooked around a throat, the other holding it up at the waist. What she was doing was suggestive, almost lascivious, like she was about to enjoy a good lick, a meal of itself. The blond hair hung limp from the head of the demon's hostage.

Alison's eyes were closed, and she did not move, leaving Arch to wonder, the demon's elbow ready to break his neck, if they had already killed his wife.

Chapter 9

Hendricks felt the world get hazy around him, his breaths coming in short, sharp bursts, the feeling of the slaps to his chest making him wonder how many more he could take without his sternum breaking. It was a steady, dull ache in his chest now, with sharp stings where the flesh had been broken. The smell of sweat was thick in his nose, and it wasn't the sweat and night smells he'd been hoping for when he'd left the bar. The demons were all around him, fanned out in a casual semi-circle, and he was at the center.

The one that was holding him had him in a tight grip, and the others were just standing back, smirking, watching. They all looked like grunge, like something he'd seen at the St. Croix County Fair when he was young. They were having a lot of fun, too, watching him as the one that had him was readying another slap, a good, hard one that would probably start the blood flowing in earnest.

It came as a little bit of a surprise to him when the arm that was holding him burst into dark flames, a quick-burning fire that didn't sear him at all. He fell but caught himself, rolling away when the hand that had been wrapped around his throat released him, consumed by hellfire, burnt to less than ashes as the soul occupying that flesh was dragged with a scream to some unimaginable pit that Hendricks really didn't ever want to have to imagine. Ever.

Standing in his place was that redhead, Starling, the one he'd seen jump off an overpass and disappear. That didn't happen normally, in his experience, and the fact that she'd just sent a demon back to the bowels of hell raised his eyebrow, too. That she'd saved his bacon was a welcome byproduct. He decided to show his gratitude by taking advantage of the breathing room she'd given him to yank his sword out of the scabbard. The remaining demons were staring at her, shell-shocked, trying to figure out who she was and what she was doing. She just looked back at all of them in the semi-circle, hands at her side, like she was waiting for them to come at her.

Her eyes were dark, and since she was right in the middle of them, Hendricks would have bet that they'd be pivoting back and forth, trying to keep an eye on all of them. If they were, he couldn't tell, because her eyes were a special sort of dark, and the parking lot of the Sinbad didn't help, what with the distinct lack of illumination and the sun sinking below the horizon. While the demons were trying to figure out what to make of her, Hendricks stabbed out and pierced the back of the one to his right, spearing right between the ribs and into the heart of the thing. It shrieked and was swallowed in a burst of flame, sounding like an infinite scream to his ears but it probably lasted only a second or less.

He stepped closer to Starling, putting himself next to her shoulder and brandishing the sword. He operated on the principle of "The enemy of my enemy is my friend," and hoped that in this case it wasn't going to bite him in the ass too hard. It really didn't matter if it did, though, because if she hadn't already shown up to save said ass, it wouldn't even have been there to be bit later.

"Thanks," he said to her, and she gave him a glance that he could only see by the subtle turn of her head, then both of them looked back at the remaining two demons, who shared a meaningful look and turned tail, running for a car on the other side of the parking lot. One of them was leading the charge, the one wearing a Metallica T-shirt. Hendricks sort of gawked at them for a moment, almost not believing what he was seeing. "What the fuck? They're running?"

"Cowards always run when the odds turn against their favor," Starling said, her voice echoing in the silence next to him. He could hear the footfalls of the runners, taking off into the distance as they reached their car and started it. She turned her head to look at him now, her red hair catching the glow of the setting sun. "Are you well?"

Hendricks tried to cut through the fuzz of the booze and the beating he'd just taken to interpret her words. Kind of old-timey, obscure, but the meaning was clear. "Well enough," he said, feeling the sting on his chest where that bastard had damned near cracked him open. "Oh, shit."

He ran for his room door as he heard the demons' tires squeal and tear ass out of the parking lot. Erin was still there, head against the frame, eyes rolled back in her head. "Aw, damn, Erin," he said, dropping to his knees and slinging his sword back into the scabbard.

Her eyes fluttered as he touched her cheek, and she looked at him for a second with a weak smile. “Mmm,” she mumbled, almost contentedly. “Was it good for you?” She seemed to settle back into unconsciousness after that, which left him feeling a bit cold.

He heard the crunch of gravel behind him and turned his head to see Starling standing there, looking down on them coldly. “She took a hell of a hit to the head,” he said, fingers reaching up into her hair to find the place where she’d hit the door frame, a little cut that was trailing blood down her face.

“She’s fine,” Starling said, like she was pronouncing the weather.

“Oh, you’re a doctor as well as a demon slayer, huh?” Hendricks didn’t deign to cast her a look. Gratitude only went so far, and she was treading on his patience now. Starling didn’t answer, and after another minute, a thought clicked through Hendricks’s drunken haze. “They were looking for me.”

“Yes,” Starling answered without pause.

“They knew where to find me,” Hendricks said again, looking up from Erin to see Starling looking down at him, a simple nod following that, and causing his blood, which had been running hot, ready for a fight, to go cold. “Oh, shit. Arch.”

*

Arch wasn’t much for swearing, but he’d heard Reeve once use the phrase, “Up to my ass in alligators,” and thought it was pretty apt for the situation. Naked, pushed against a wall by a demon with his face mashed so he could only see out of one eye, and that one eye was fixated on his wife, who was hanging limp in the arms of a demon woman who was putting a tongue in her ear.

Arch was a man who knew his weaknesses, and one of them was his temper. Not with Alison, not ever. But his teammates had seen it on the football field from time to time, and when it came out, the common consensus he’d heard muttered is that they were glad he was on their side.

A breath of air surged into his lungs, fueled entirely by rage. He let out a yell that caused the hands that had him gripped to loosen, probably from surprise. Arch pulled his face down the drywall, causing it to peel skin from his cheek. He shifted his weight forward, demon on his back, elbow on the back of his neck, and caused the man to dip lower as Arch dropped into a football stance against the wall. The foul thing lost its balance, and Arch could feel the thing's jeans and t-shirt fall against his naked back. He didn't like it there, but it wasn't going to be there for long.

Arch launched off the balls of his feet, like he was tackling the wall. He managed to drop enough of the demon between his shoulder and the drywall to pin the man in place as he slammed through, smashing the demon into the two by fours and cushioning the blow to himself. Using the demon as a buffer, he plowed on, drawing screams from it as he ran it straight through the support frames and heard them snap. Arch stopped, getting back to his feet enough to see the studs in the wall were broken and that the demon was resting on them, just ready to be impaled, if Arch could pull it off.

He came down with all his weight and slammed the demon, battering him down. There was a scream, then a hiss, as Arch pushed as hard as he'd pushed on any weight ever in his life. He heard a squealing sound, like air being let out of a tire, and realized it came from the demon, that there was a little bit of the stud poking through his chest.

The demon burst into shadowed flames, head to toe, and Arch had only a moment to revel in his good work when another of them slammed into him from behind and carried him through the shattered wall into the bathroom.

*

Starling was driving, but she didn't look too happy about it, the first real emotion he'd caught from her. They'd stashed Erin in Hendricks's motel room, splayed out on the bed, unconscious and mumbling. She'd be fine, Hendricks was pretty sure, finer than Arch was anyway, if his suspicions were right. When Hendricks had asked if Starling had a car, she'd shrugged, so he'd grabbed Erin's keys—which she'd gotten back from Phil grudgingly after promising she was walking straight to the motel—off her belt, and he'd run drunkenly back to the bar, Starling following along much more gracefully.

It had taken a few minutes for Starling to get the car in drive, and Hendricks was having to give her lessons on how to drive, which should have alarmed him, but didn't. He was feeling the pull of sleep, wishing he was back in bed, freshly laid and ready to embrace the exhaustion that was tugging at him. Instead he was in pain from the damage to his chest, stiff in all the wrong places, and the woman who was next to him was not the one he'd been wanting to spend his evening with. Nothing wrong with Starling, but the woman was so cold he suspected his dick would freeze if it got anywhere near the presumed gap between her legs.

"This is... not bad," Starling said, presumably making a pronouncement about the experience of driving rather than her performance at it. She had her hands where he'd told her to put them, at ten and two. Or rather, where he'd helped her position them, because she didn't know what he meant when he said, "At ten and two." Her hands had been cold like they'd been sitting in the freezer, which just gave him more grounds for the suspicion that she'd chill his cock if he ever got it near her. Erin was warm, though. And unconscious, which he was quick to blame himself for (and might have been even more of a douser to his libido than Starling).

They sped along the highway toward Midian's downtown, Starling tugging the wheel a little more than was necessary. It was causing the car to—not quite swerve, but close. "Whoa," Hendricks said. "Take it easy." She gave him an inquiring look, and he knew she had no clue what he was saying. "With the wheel. Don't jerk it so much to correct. Be gentle with it." Starling corrected the next time in a much smoother manner, and he nodded approval. "How did you know they were coming for me?"

"Word spreads," she said coolly, as she did everything else.

"Well, thanks for the help," he said, trying to push the gratitude before the next thing he was going to say. "But didn't it occur to you to mention that they might also be going after Arch?"

She didn't look up from the road before speaking. "My concern was you, not anyone else. In this, I fulfilled my aims."

"Don't think I'm not appreciative," Hendricks said, "but I'm not the only one in this particular fight." He paused as they came into the town, Starling riding the brakes harder than she needed to before they came upon a stop sign. "Mind telling me what this is all about? You show up before, all mysterious, and—" He looked back as a red and blue light flashed through the cab. "Shit. Pull over." He looked back and waved her to the side of the road. "Pull over."

"Why?" She gazed at him with wonder, like she was genuinely curious.

He stared back at her. "Because that's what we do when a cop pulls up behind us with lights on."

She stared back, impassive, as she guided the car to the shoulder. "I thought we were going to save the other police officer?"

Hendricks took a breath. "Yeah, that was the sentiment. Unfortunately, I don't know where he lives."

She cocked an eyebrow at him but had no time to say anything else before there was a knock at the window. Starling stared for a moment at the door before Hendricks gestured toward the mechanism and Starling rolled it down.

"You must be Sheriff Reeve," Hendricks said, before the man could say a word. He was older, balding, a little paunchy. Hendricks hadn't talked to Arch about his job much, but the way the man wore his seniority, he had the feel of a guy in charge. Hendricks hadn't even caught the name from Arch; it had been plastered all over campaign posters in the town square that had yet to be removed.

"Yeah," Reeve said, leaning over just slightly to look at Hendricks. "And?"

"Sorry," Hendricks said. "We were just on our way to see Arch."

Reeve gave them a perplexed look, narrowed eyes and all. "And you're doing this in one of my deputies' cars because?"

"We're just visiting town," Hendricks said, trying to lay it on smooth, "and I was drinking with Erin over at Fast Freddie's. Well, she had a little too much, so she's sleeping it off over at my motel. I gotta go talk to Arch, though, I was supposed to meet up with him after his shift was done at three and I think we missed connecting because I ended up hanging out with Erin—" Hendricks was talking as fast as he could, trying to show he was a little wasted. It played into the next part of his plan.

"That's a real fine story," Reeve said, and Hendricks could tell he was weighing all the stuff that had just come out. There was definitely a heavy air of doubt, like the man didn't want to accept what was being said at face value. Hendricks suspected he had the run of the man, though; loyalty would mean something to him, and dropping the names of two of his deputies would at least give Hendricks some breathing room. Maybe. "But you were still doing fifty in a thirty-five." He gazed from Hendricks to Starling. "And swerving. Ma'am, have you had anything to drink?"

Starling cocked her head at him, still serious. "No."

Hendricks could tell she was ready to say something else, but he stopped her. "She's my designated driver."

"Uh huh," Reeve said, staring down at them. "Tell you what," he seemed to decide. "We'll head on over to Arch's, see what he has to say about all this."

"That sounds great," Hendricks said with a smile. "You mind leading the way? I'm pretty wasted and she doesn't know this town for shit."

Reeve gave him something just short of a leer—trying to keep the politeness on until he knew for fact that Hendricks was a lying scumbag. "All right," was the measured response that came back, but the implication it carried was, *Fuck you. Try and run and I will own your ass for all time.*

Hendricks gestured for Starling to roll up the window and start the engine. They waited in silence as the red-and-blue lights flashed past them, going slow, and after a moment Starling brought the car back on the road to follow the police cruiser.

*

Arch rolled into the bathroom, managing to turn the tables on the demon that was on him like a duck on a June bug, slamming the thing's head into the bathroom sink. It bared its teeth at him, demon teeth, like pointed canines you'd see on a vampire in a movie. He brought its head down toward him in a sudden jerk after holding it back for just a moment, and let it clip the top of its head on the sink. He heard the cracking of the ceramic countertop, the demon's face looked dazed, and he drove it back toward him again with so much force that the lip of the counter broke with the impact and the demon went limp for a moment.

It was all Arch needed to get a leg up and shove the thing, hard, into the shower curtain, where it got entangled. He got to his feet and pulled the shattered bowl of the sink out of the small pedestal, holding it like an awkward baseball bat, water spraying out of the plumbing at him. He took the whole thing and swung like a champ at the demon just getting up from the tub. He aimed at the neck, figuring it was the weakest part of the whole body. The sink shattered upon impact, raining fragments into Arch's unprotected skin. He was rewarded with a hiss like the one he'd heard before, then the room was lit up by a flare of orange light. The thing disappeared in a burst of dark flame, leaving behind the smell of sulfur and brimstone.

The sink was ruined but Arch didn't give a damn. He looked for a weapon and came up with the shower rod, since the sink was too fragmented to do him much good. The rod was already ripped out of the wall from where the demon had torn it down in landing, and he readied himself for the last of them, the woman, whom he could hear out in the kitchen still, and he saw red thinking about what she might be doing to Alison. If Alison was even still alive. He felt a lurch in his stomach and started toward the door. As he passed the gargantuan hole in the wall, he looked out and saw the switchblade just waiting on the carpet up ahead.

"Did you get him?" came a female voice, kind of husky, and he couldn't remember her name. Severson? Amanda, maybe?

"Yeah," Arch said, lowering his voice, making himself cough. "I got him." He wanted to be wearing clothes, but this wasn't the moment, not with what was at stake. All hell had broken loose upon his house, his home, and he could feel the rage covering all the aches and pains that ought to be wearing on him. He wondered if anyone would have called the Sheriff's Department yet. One of his neighbors was elderly, the woman below him. Doubtful she'd hear much of anything but *Wheel of Fortune* at this time of night. The ones on the other side of his kitchen were younger, though, and from out of town originally. They might call 911 if they heard what was happening in his place.

"Let's get them out of here, then," came the voice of the female demon. He was almost certain her name was Amanda. He remembered the mug shot. "Hollywood's waiting."

Arch pondered his course. "Gimme a hand," he said, rough and low. He heard movement out in the kitchen, footsteps coming toward him along with something being gently set down on the floor outside. He hoped it was Alison. He hoped Amanda wasn't giving much thought to his request, that she was dumb. He was betting on that, actually. Smart people generally didn't become common criminals, after all. If they went to crime at all, they generally became uncommon ones.

He saw her turn the corner at the door and come in, not even bothering to be cautious. He wondered if she was high right now, strung out on something that could make a demon dulled and slow. She twitched in surprise when she saw him, but he was already coming at her, driving the end of the shower rod into her midsection. It didn't pierce the skin, probably because it was too dull, but then, he hadn't meant it to. Arch ran her as hard as he could forward, and she fell back, pushed into the bedroom door that was directly opposite the bathroom.

While she was falling, Arch leapt sideways through the hole in the wall, diving for the switchblade. He came up with it after face planting, hard. He wasn't a martial artist, more of a brawler, so rolling wasn't something that came naturally to him, but he didn't care. He had the blade and he was turned around, coming to his feet in a lunge toward the bedroom door.

He caught a furious look from Amanda as she rounded the corner heading for him, a serious mad-on coming through the haze of whatever she was on. The blade caught her beneath the sternum and it slid in as her anger turned to surprise. Arch was face to face with her but he dropped to his knees and put all his weight into it as he slid down, ripping the knife into where her guts would be. She stared down at him, kneeling before her in his nakedness, a stunned look on her face, like she couldn't believe she'd gotten gutted by a nude black man. It lasted for about a second before the flames broke loose, starting at the place where he'd torn her open, progressing swiftly over the exterior of her body and flaring in her eyes and mouth as she screamed her way back to oblivion.

Exhausted, all his adrenaline blown out in one good burst, Arch fell back and crawled on his hands and knees to the kitchen, to Alison, and picked up her head and clutched it against him. He was listening for breath, and when he finally heard it, he thanked his God in a whisper that was ragged with worry and relief.

, *

"How do you think he's doing?" Hendricks asked, more to cut the nervous tension in the car than because he thought she'd be able to tell him. He didn't want to be responsible for someone else, which was why he'd never taken on a partner in the demon-hunting game. It didn't have to be a solitary occupation, after all, and lots of people liked to team up on either a short or long-term basis. That wasn't for him. He knew there were others like him, too, loners, and he could read the looks in their eyes. No entanglements, that was the rule. Just blow around from hotspot to hotspot, doing their thing, not having to worry if anyone else got hurt. It was sweet enough, for a while.

Starling didn't look at him as she answered. "Fighting a demon without a blessed weapon puts a heavy burden upon your friend."

"He's not my friend," Hendricks said out of rote habit. When Starling looked over at him, her face close-guarded silence and accusation, he elaborated. "I don't have any friends."

"You seemed friendly enough with the woman who was with you outside your dwelling." There was no accusation there, just a flat tone, a statement of fact. He thought.

"That's a different kind of friendly, Miss Starling. A whole different kind."

*

Arch had caught her steady breathing now, like she was just asleep, and when he pinched her hand he saw her eyelids flutter, which was a good thing, he remembered from his first aid training. She let out a soft moan and he tried to gather an explanation of what he was going say to her when she woke up. It wasn't going to be a fun explanation, he knew that much. He was considering the fact that he hadn't heard a mess of sirens to be a mark in his favor, but then he looked out the window and saw the flash of red and blue, and he had a feeling his night might actually be about to get worse.

*

They pulled into a parking lot for a duplex apartment building, a small one that looked like it maybe had four units all together—two upstairs, two downstairs, with the doors to each of them obvious on the front of the building. One of the doors was blown clear open, off its hinges, which

Hendricks generally considered a bad sign. "Too late," he muttered. "Fuck."

Starling shifted the car into neutral before figuring out how to put it in park, and the sheriff was already out of his car by the time Hendricks staggered out the passenger door of his. "Hands in the air!" Reeve shouted at Hendricks, who complied quickly. He had turned his back on the door to the second-floor apartment, probably trying to make sure that there wasn't a threat at his back before he dealt with the possibility of one at his front. Hendricks kept his hands up then glanced to Starling, who was also out of the car, her red hair slung over one shoulder like it had been braided there. Her hands were not remotely up, and Reeve had taken notice of that. The sheriff's gun came around accordingly, and Hendricks got a bad feeling about what was about to happen.

"Hold it," came a shout from the second floor, and Reeve turned his head just for a second to take in the sight of Arch, wearing only his work pants, running across the balcony toward the stairs on the right side of the building. The whole place was an older brick building, with redwood for the guardrails across the balcony. It gave the place a different feel, a little homey, a little woodsy, even though it was only a block or two from the center of town. "It's all right, sir," Arch said, coming down the steps.

Reeve gave him an *Are you fucking kidding me?* look but held his tongue. Hendricks just stood there and waited, wondering how best to avoid the conflicting stories that were about to come pouring out in an attempt to untangle this mess that was sitting in front of them. He didn't like the thought of that, not one bit, and would probably have been quicker about finding a way out of it if not for the fact that he was still very, very drunk, and the sway in his head made him acutely aware of it.

"I need you to put out an APB on that small-timer, Amanda Severson," Arch said, now crossing the parking lot toward them. "She and her little friends just busted up my place."

Hendricks was impressed, then he realized that Arch probably wasn't even lying about that, what with his door being broken open and all. It made him wonder if the big man had driven them off singlehandedly, then made him wonder how many of them he'd tussled with.

"Severson?" Reeve asked, putting his gun back in the holster. "Medium height? Dark hair? Got picked up for intent to distribute a few months back?"

Arch nodded, not even taking in or acknowledging Hendricks yet. "That's the one. She and three others just broke down my door, looked like they made to stage a home invasion."

Reeve gave a quick look over around the parking lot, like he couldn't believe it. The sun wasn't even setting yet. "We don't exactly have a long history of daring daylight break-ins in the center of Midian. And certainly not by criminals who would be dumb enough to pick out the residence of a known member of the sheriff's department."

"Yet that's exactly what happened," Arch said, eyes boring into the sheriff's. Hendricks just watched, transfixed. "I beat 'em up pretty good, think I shot a couple of 'em , but they bum rushed me. Might have been wearing Kevlar, because I didn't see 'em bleed at all. This was something I ain't never seen before, just crazy. They knocked out Alison, that Severson woman laid hands on her."

Reeve got serious, real serious, fast. "She all right?"

Arch's voice went low. "She's a little hazy, needs to go to the doctor, I think. But I drove 'em off. Was about to call for help when you pulled up." He cast a look to Hendricks. "Good to see you, Hendricks. Sorry I didn't catch up with you earlier."

"It's all right," Hendricks said, giving Arch a knowing look. "I was just spending some time with Erin when some other friends of ours showed up unexpectedly. Starling and I hung out with them for a bit until they left, but Erin was a little too far gone by that point and passed out." He tried to figure out the best way to phrase things to communicate information without making it a dead giveaway to Reeve that there was subtext. He tried to make his look pained, and found it came pretty easily. He was still hiding a hell of an injury under his coat, after all. "Bet you wish you'd brought your wife out with us, huh?"

Arch didn't smile in his reply. "I need to get her to the hospital, get her looked at." He looked to Reeve. "You want to get this place cordoned off for me?"

If the sheriff took umbrage to being given an order by his deputy, he didn't show it. "Damned right," he said. "I'll get that APB sent out, too, call in all the boys. We'll find these fuckers and drag 'em in by the short hairs, leave nothing left but a bald and bleeding patch by the time we're done. No one does this shit to the law in Calhoun County."

*

Hollywood stroked his forehead, leaning back against the chair in the old dairy farmer's house. It was beyond inconvenient, having to be here now, but since he'd killed that chambermaid in Chattanooga, it would probably be more of a hindrance for him to stay there. There weren't that many five-star hotels in a town like that, after all, and if he'd been in one, it was unlikely that the next would be much better. Fuck Southern hospitality.

He pulled his hand back from his brow. And then there was this. Krauther stood in front of him, looking a little contrite, one lone lackey still in tow. "So …" Hollywood said, "how'd they die?"

"Some woman," Krauther said, "some woman or some thing, I'm not sure. She felt like …" Krauther's essence flared behind the veneer, and Hollywood could see it—see him—like he was looking through a thick glass at something distorted on the other side. "I don't know what she felt like. Maybe—"

"One of ours?" Hollywood tossed out, still rubbing his forehead. He was throbbing, all through his essence, so much annoyance that he couldn't give form to. After all, there were only so many more of his kind in this pointless burg, only so many demons that would be willing to hitch their star to his, and if he made an example out of these two fuck-ups, that was two less he'd have available to send to their horrible deaths later, if needed. He took a deep breath of the cowshit-filled air in the parlor of the old farmhouse. And if all this came to fruition, there would damned sure be a need for that later.

"I don't know," Krauther said, and Hollywood looked up to see the fear flare in his essence. "One of *theirs*, maybe."

"One of THEIRS?" Hollywood was on his feet in a second, Krauther's Metallica t-shirt twisted up in his hand, the demon holding on by the balls of his feet to the floor as Hollywood had him unbalanced. "Tell me you don't fucking think one of THEIRS is here, now?"

Krauther's eyes were wide, and his arms were wiggling, trying to keep him from tipping over. "I … I don't know, Hollywood. She had a vibe, man. Power. Essence, maybe. Not sure what the deal is, but she didn't have the smell of a human."

Hollywood let Krauther go, let him fall flat on his ass. His mind was racing, faster than it usually did, even when he did a snort of blow. Sometimes it amazed him that human drugs worked on demons, but the shell was the same, really; the essence was the big difference. Humans had no souls, not really, just little things, comparatively speaking. But his kind—and the others … they were full up. Bursting out of their bodies. Not like a human, which was almost an empty vessel.

"Maybe she was just another interested party," Hollywood said at last, looking from Krauther to the other minion then to Sleeveless, who waited in the corner, watching the whole thing. "This is a hotspot, after all, there's plenty of draw here. It could have been one of the Commission, trying to keep you from outing yourselves. No reason to think one …" He didn't grind his teeth, but only because he smiled instead, "… one of *their* kind would be about. They don't get out and about that much anymore." He smoothed his tie and looked down at Krauther. "Have you ever even seen one of them?"

Krauther hesitated before answering. "No."

Hollywood smirked. Fucking stupid hick. The excitable type, ready to jump to crazy conclusions with no reason to go there except the meth. Figured. "It wasn't one of them. You smelled it wrong. Maybe a stray demon, maybe a half-human. Their kind doesn't come down here anymore." He straightened his tie again, tightened it up, then looked back toward Sleeveless. "Time?"

Sleeveless pulled out his cell phone. "Eight o'clock."

"Okay." Hollywood straightened his collar, too. "We got a little time to kill before our other team checks in." There was a little nervous tension there, and he didn't like it. Whoever this woman was, she couldn't have gotten to both teams, could she? No. The other one, the cop, they'd be bringing him along any minute. Him and his wife.

Hollywood put it out of his mind and compulsively turned to a mirror that was on the wall, a garish thing with the brand of a major beer printed on the middle of it, like the wicked queen's image was a reflection of a Miller Lite logo. He looked at himself in the mirror, smoothed his hair back into place in the slicked-back ponytail then checked his clothing. Flawless. He cast a glance at Sleeveless. "Just to be safe, prep the alternates, will you?" One couldn't be too careful, when dealing with meth-addled idiots, after all.

Sleeveless nodded and disappeared into the hallway behind them. There was the sound of a door opening, then footsteps on stairs. A few seconds later, there was a sound of screaming—urgent, crying, terrified. As it should be.

Hollywood stared in the mirror, past the brand name of the beer. It was like it didn't even exist if he concentrated hard enough. All that was left in there was him. Him and what he was about to bring upon the world. Because he was worthy. Because he was the one. The one with the vision to do it. He looked at the flawless, even teeth staring back at him and recognized once again that there was a reason he had been passed over in the past, why he'd failed at acting and chosen to transition into producing. It was that vision which would carry him through. All that was standing between him and it was execution. And finally, he'd get what he'd deserved all along.

A starring role.

*

Creampuff was quiet, now. That was a thankful thing, at least for Ygrusibas. Being winnowed in the pits of fire for the last eight or ten millennia (it was hard to keep track) was one thing. Being trapped in the body of a cow was quite another. Creampuff might have taken umbrage to that, but by this point in the summoning process, there just wasn't that much of Creampuff left. Maybe an instinct or two, but otherwise, Ygrusibas was running just about the entire show.

Which should have been more eventful than it was. Ygrusibas was neither he nor she, but a transcendence of the mortal two genders, encompassing both. Yet somehow, it was trapped in a body that was decidedly binary. This was unfortunate but could be remedied with time and some effort. The change would require energy that was presently being expended to build up strength, though, which was a curious thing.

The gate was still an insurmountable obstacle, but Ygrusibas was not impressed. Millennia of imprisonment in the pits of fire compared to a day in the pasture? It was a welcome change, it told itself, over and over. No roasting flesh, no torment that ran soul deep. This was positively… well, *boring* by comparison, which might have been part of the problem.

Ygrusibas had grown accustomed to torment, had survived it by plotting, by thinking of all who would suffer once it had been freed, given release from said torment. Anger and bitterness were the flames in Ygrusibas's soul that had seen it through. With the external flames gone, the inner ones burned all the brighter, and with them came a desire to make things happen.

But none of it was happening fast enough. The body that Ygrusibas had taken was still trapped in a pasture, in a prison built just for this sort of animal. All attempts to break through the fence had resulted in a special kind of pain that Creampuff (or what was left of her) had predicted with a sort of dim-witted amusement. Ygrusibas hadn't found it nearly so amusing, though. It was almost as bad as the pits again.

And so Ygrusibas seethed as sundown approached, casting the farmhouse in the distance in a fire-red glow that reminded Ygrusibas of where it had so recently escaped from. This did not sit well, not at all, even as the second night came on, and the demon waited for its full strength to return. Because when it did, the earth would tremble.

When it did, the world would end.

Chapter 10

Alison walked out of the emergency room under her own power a little before midnight, Arch at her side. Hendricks breathed a little sigh of relief when he saw them, sitting where he was on the hood of Erin's car, almost sober by now. He had a few things on his mind, not the least of which was Erin herself. He and Starling had gone back to the hotel to make sure the deputy was all right. She was; she'd even had a half-awake conversation with Hendricks while he'd cleaned the cut on the side of her head. It was a little thing, just a scratch, but there'd definitely be a bruise there tomorrow.

"Erin all right?" Arch asked as soon as he got within range of Hendricks.

"She's fine," Hendricks responded, giving Mrs. Stan a polite smile. "How do you do, ma'am?" He tipped his hat to her.

"I'm all right," Alison said then shot a look at her husband before returning it to Hendricks. "And you are?"

"This is Lafayette Hendricks, dear," Arch said tightly. "He's an old friend, in town trying to settle some business."

Hendricks couldn't have put it much better himself. He tipped his hat again to Alison then turned back to Arch. "And there is some serious business that needs settling."

Arch nodded, his uniform looking just a bit disheveled. Hendricks hadn't seen his uniform disheveled even after the dust up with the demons at MacGruder's farm. He assumed it was something of a new situation for Arch. "I never did catch your friend's name," Arch said, looking to Starling, who stood with her arms folded only a few feet away.

"He doesn't have any friends," Starling said, matter-of-factly. "I am Starling."

Arch sent a look Hendricks's way. *Really?* was how Hendricks interpreted it. "And you're a … hunter as well?"

She cocked her head at him, but her expression didn't change. "No."

Arch gave Hendricks another look, and Hendricks felt a little swell of pity. He hadn't figured out Starling's angle either, but she'd been damned helpful and damned quiet, so he hadn't pressed her too hard about what she was up to. Yet. "What's the move?"

"I'm dropping Alison off at her parents' house," Arch announced, drawing a surprised look from Alison herself. "Then we need to have a discussion with those boys out at MacGruder's."

"Arch," Alison said, softly, like she didn't want Starling and Hendricks to hear her, "what are you talking about? What about our apartment?"

"Whole place is trashed," Arch said. "Not really in a fit state for you to sleep there tonight."

Hendricks saw the questioning look Mrs. Stan gave her husband, then the polite gaze coupled with a smile that she turned his and Starling's way. It wasn't a uniquely Southern belle thing, the facade over the desire to argue, but Hendricks thought Southern women did it better than almost anyone. Most of the Yankee girls back home would just fight it out with their man in public, not even giving a fuck who saw.

"Arch," Alison said again, this time with an unmistakable trace of steel underneath, "I really think you should come with me." She said it politely, but the edge was there, and it was all order.

The big man brushed it off like all he heard was the text, no subtext. "No. I'm a deputy sheriff, and I'm not letting the bastards behind this get brought in by anyone else. This is my responsibility."

Hendricks just felt sorry for them now, the both of them, because Arch didn't give a damn, wasn't listening, and Alison was all polite embarrassment for his sake. She turned back to Hendricks, gave him a flushed, *Excuse-me-while-I-beat-some-sense-into-my-wayward-idiot-of-a-husband* look and rounded on Arch to hook her arm in his and presumably move him out of earshot.

Arch resisted, though, and looked to Hendricks. "I'm gonna drop her off. Her folks are on the outskirts. Meet back at your motel in a half hour or so?"

Hendricks felt the tug of discomfort, suspecting he knew that Arch was gonna get an earful when he stepped into his car. "Sure thing," he said and nodded at Starling, who started toward the driver's side of Erin's car again. "I'll drive this time."

Starling shrugged, handing him the keys as they crossed at the hood. She looked at Arch's receding back, Alison's arm crooked in his, and studied them as though she were looking at something peculiar. Neither of them was speaking, but their body language was all stiff, and not just from the fight they'd both been in. Hendricks could see it—could see it and was glad he wasn't riding with them now.

"She is greatly unhappy with him," Starling observed, opening her door, but never looking away from the couple as they made their way through the parking lot toward the police cruiser in the distance.

Hendricks watched them as they got into the Explorer, saw Alison open her mouth then, saw the first words start to spill out with the flagrant gestures, her hands waving, finger pointing, and he started the car. He took one last look as he turned the wheel of the subcompact and took it out of the parking space, headed toward the exit, before he'd even fastened his safety belt. "You ain't even shitting about that."

*

Arch didn't really want to hear it, but he had a vague inkling that he was going to get an earful as soon as the car door was shut. It didn't even take that long, actually, before Alison blew up at him.

"—can't believe you'd just dump me off at my parents house after that!" She was railing good, letting him have it, and he would probably have been more moved if he wasn't itching to just lay waste to demons, split their fleshy bellies open and send them back to hell. He had the switchblade in his pocket and he was jonesing to use it again, to turn it loose on that Hollywood bastard.

"Sorry," Arch said, sensing an opening and cutting her off. "Those guys, the ones that broke into our apartment? They've got friends. They're not gonna stop."

Alison was quiet for a beat. She got like that, every so often. If you knew her, it wasn't hard to imagine her as the salutatorian of her class, but it was easy to pass her off at first blush as just some ditz. Arch might have made that mistake himself if he hadn't known her since grade school. She didn't cultivate a thoughtful persona and was prone to gushing. "You're saying they aren't going to let off coming after us until … what? You're dead?"

"Seems likely," Arch said, backing the Explorer out of the space and putting it in drive. He eased through the hospital parking lot, as though expecting a demon to come jumping out from behind a parked car. None did, and he reached the edge of the lot and took the cruiser out onto the highway.

"So you're going to go after them and stop it?" He knew she was staring at him, and he didn't want to fuel any fears she might have. "You and that cowboy? And his …" He could see her frown out of the corner of his eye. "… girlfriend or whatever?" She seemed to think about it. "That wasn't his girlfriend. I'd swear they were just strangers, standing next to each other like they were." Arch grunted and Alison leaned toward him. "Why aren't you taking Reeve and the boys with you? Why are you working with some hired-hand cowboy that no one knows?" She let the silence of his unanswered question hang there between them, and he couldn't think up anything fast enough. "What are you not telling me, Arch?"

"These guys are bad news," Arch said. "Badder than anything Reeve would suspect."

"And you gotta deal with them?" Alison said, skeptical. The headlights bounced down the highway, illuminating it under the cloudy Tennessee night. "Why not the state police? Or the FBI, if Reeve isn't up for it?"

Arch shook his head. "This is a local problem now. Not something they'd handle." He wanted to tell her more, but how would he even start to explain it, let alone give her the depth of reassurance she'd need after he broke it to her that he was going after demons? "It'll be okay. This cowboy, he's good. Real good. Used to be in the Marine Corps, and he knows these scumbags. How they think. What they'll do." He gave her a cautious smile. "We'll get 'em wrapped up, and then you and I can get back to the business of living our lives." He couldn't quite smile at this because somewhere deep he knew he was lying, that there was no going back after what he'd learned the last couple days. It was like his whole world had opened up, like something had showed itself to him that he'd always known was lurking out there under the surface. Like he'd been waiting for someone to tell him what Hendricks had finally come out and said.

Demons walked among humans. They were out there, they were

scheming, and human beings were nothing but prey for them.

He gave Alison another tense smile as the Explorer kicked into a higher gear. He looked at the speedometer, and realized he was going seventy in a fifty-five. He flipped on the lights and gunned the accelerator even more. He'd killed four of them by himself, some with his hands and what he'd had nearby, and Hendricks had said that just didn't happen. He wanted to do it again, and soon. And when he was done with them, well …

… he wasn't sure he really wanted to be done.

*

Hendricks opened the door to the motel and let himself in. He checked on Erin, whom he had covered up with a blanket. She was sleeping and had turned a little to face the window. She did not stir as he came in, and he brushed the hair out of her eyes. She was so peaceful he didn't want to disturb her. Her little frame had curled up, almost in the fetal position, only not quite there, like she wanted to hug her knees to her chest. The air conditioner was working better tonight, keeping the heat in the room to a minimum, and the smell of the musty air it put out filled the small room.

Hendricks walked to the sink and took off his coat, laying it across a chair by the closet. "Come in," he said to Starling, who was lingering just inside the door, looking over the room like it was some curiosity to be examined. "Shut the door behind you, please?" She did and then stood back and watched him in the mirror as he hung that hat up on the hook on the closet door then peeled his ripped and bloody shirt off. He'd kept his coat closed while Arch and the sheriff had been around, hoping they were too distracted to comment on it. It wasn't as hot tonight, anyway. Which was a way of saying it was still hot, just maybe not as hot as it had been. It had worked, plainly, because neither bothered to get him to open it, which was good. Because even before he'd taken the shirt off, it was plain that things were not as they were supposed to be.

There was heavy bruising in the middle of his chest, across his pectorals, and it had hurt when he'd spread his arms to take off his coat. Even more when he'd taken off the shirt. He gently touched the center of the mess, where five different spots oozed blood that had been staunched by the cloth. When he ripped it free, they came loose again and started bleeding once more. He grabbed Kleenex from the dispenser on the counter and blotted at them, trying to stop the flow.

"You are wounded," Starling said, now just behind him.

"You don't miss much, do you?" Hendricks said, blanching at the pain as he looked back at her in the mirror. "Seems like you state the obvious a lot."

"I say what I see," Starling replied.

"And not much else," Hendricks agreed. He turned to face her, still holding the tissue tight against his chest. "So who are you?"

There was no register of emotion from her. "Starling."

"Well, that's a name," Hendricks said. "But unless you're about to grow a set of wings and go flapping around the room, it doesn't tell me shit about who you really are, what you're really here for."

She cocked her head at him. "Wings?"

He started to raise an eyebrow at her but stopped. He couldn't decide if she was being deliberately dense or just evasive. Better to avoid the sarcasm and just try a different tack. "So, why are you here?"

"To keep you from getting killed," she said simply, like it was obvious. "And to bring you a message."

He stared her down. "Same one as last time?

She nodded. "You do not even know why you are here. Not yet."

He leaned against the wall, more for support than to look cool, though he kind of hoped he did. "So, why don't you tell me?"

"I cannot," she said with a simple shake of the head.

"Of course not," Hendricks said and shuffled over to his duffel, digging into the side, where he kept the first aid kit. "Because that might be helpful, giving me knowledge I can use to help in the job I'm doing."

"The task you have before you is not the task you are called to perform," she said, a little singsong-y about it. He stared at her in the mirror as he carefully removed a long bandage and some medical tape from the kit, along with a few sterile swabs that he tore from their packaging. "You came because she told you to come, because she sensed the emanations of this place and thought it important, more important than any of the other locations she could have sent you to. She was correct," Starling said drily, "but not for the reasons she thinks, and not for the ones she has told you."

"Uh huh," Hendricks said, and ran the first swab across his chest, feeling the alcohol burn as he did it. “You realize if you hadn’t saved my ass earlier tonight, I’d be madder than hell at you for being so damned irritating in drip-feeding me this vague bullshit?” He placed a piece of gauze over the first of the wounds and taped it in place. “I mean, I’m a demon hunter by trade. This is what I do. Telling me there are unholy in a town is winding me up and turning me loose, no other instruction required, because I’ll find them, I’ll open their guts to the sunshine, and I’ll repeat until the hotspot simmers down and I’m off to the next demon scramble.”

He turned around and faced her. “But you start giving me this, ‘You’re not here for what you think you are’ crap and muddying the waters for me? Then you won’t tell me why I’m really here?” He took a step toward her. “Let me tell you something. I’m here to kill demons. It’s what I do. If you think I’m here for some other reason, I’m gonna have to politely tell you that you don’t know what you’re talking about.” He stood there, shirtless, for just another minute staring into Starling’s cold eyes before he went back to the sink. She did not react at all, not to anything he said.

He waited about five minutes, patching each of the wounds in turn then wrapping his whole chest in a bandage around his ribs. Once he had finished he pulled a fresh shirt from his duffel and put it on, a white one this time. He turned to say something else to Starling, but the room was empty save for Erin, asleep on the bed.

*

Arch wasn’t on familiar enough terms with his in-laws to just open the door and walk in even though he suspected it was unlocked. They hadn’t phoned ahead, after all, so he waited until the lights came on in the front window and Mr. Longholt opened the door. Arch still thought of him as Mr. Longholt even though he’d known the man for nearly ten years and had always been told to call him Bill. Longholt smiled at the sight of them on his front porch, though there was a faintly perplexed look on his face. Mr. Longholt was a good man.

And a big one, too. Just a couple inches shorter than Arch, he had been a football player himself at one time. Now he was a little larger around the middle but still powerfully built. He had an air of distinction, too; he was the sort of man who always wore a suit for the sake of propriety, though he got rid of his jacket and tie as soon he was out of his wife's sight. His hair was barely gray even now that he was closer to seventy than sixty, and a youthful twinkle in his eyes gave him a liveliness that most men his age lacked.

"Come in, come in," Longholt said, ushering them in without hesitation. It was past midnight, now, just barely, and he didn't even ask them what they were there for before getting them inside. "Addy!" Mr. Longholt shouted, down the long hall, "Arch and Ali are here!"

"Well," Mrs. Longholt's voice came back, "what are they doing here at this hour?"

Mr. Longholt smiled broadly. "Now, Addy, let us not forgot our manners," he admonished her in the mildest of tones.

Mrs. Longholt swept down the hall a moment later, clutching tightly to her bathrobe, bustling along to sweep her only daughter up in an enveloping hug then transferring it to Arch and following through with a peck on the cheek. "My manners are well remembered, Husband," she said, giving him just the hint of an evil eye. "It is always within acceptable bounds to ask your guests what they might be up to showing up at your door after midnight." Her platinum hair caught the porch light coming through the front door window. She looked like an older version of Alison, gracefully aged.

"We had a little incident earlier tonight," Arch said, after giving Alison a moment to speak in which she said nothing. "Some criminals broke down our door—"

Addy clucked at them, that sympathetic mom noise. "I always worry about y'all, with that job of yours, Arch."

"Now, Addy," Mr. Longholt said, "Arch didn't even say if they were there because of him. Don't go jumping to conclusions."

"They were there because of me," Arch said, feeling more strained than he would have liked to admit. "And I'd greatly appreciate it if Alison could stay here with you tonight while I take care of this particular problem."

Mr. Longholt exchanged a look with his wife. "Of course," he said quietly. "Without doubt."

"Thank you," Arch said and kissed Alison on the cheek. She said nothing, didn't even really turn to look at him. He waited, hesitant, for almost a minute then turned to leave.

"Well, Alison!" Addy said, perturbed, "aren't you going to bid your husband goodbye before he goes off into the night to—"

"Addy," Mr. Longholt said warningly then smiled at Arch. "I'll walk you to your car."

Alison gave Arch a rather perfunctory kiss on the cheek, just the slightest hint of affection. He couldn't find it in himself to fault her for it. After all, he wasn't up for discussing it, he hadn't allowed her to dissuade him, and he wasn't even staying long enough to get her settled in at her parents' house.

Mr. Longholt closed the door behind them, his slippered feet making quiet noises on the front walk as they made their way toward the Explorer in the drive. "She'll forgive you in time, Arch."

Arch didn't know quite what to say to that. "They broke down our door," he said after a minute. "Probably scared the living daylights out of Alison. If she blames me for all that, I couldn't fault her. I'm sure my leaving makes it worse, but I need to—"

"I know," Mr. Longholt said with a quick nod. "We need not discuss what's going to happen in any sort of detail; I'd imagine Sheriff Reeve is not in on your plans and it's probably for the better."

Arch squinted at his father-in-law, wondering just what the man was trying to say by that. Even had he not been so all-fired ready to go kill some demons, he wasn't sure he wanted to inquire too deeply into this. "These men," he said instead, "are dangerous. Guns might not stop them."

Longholt raised an eyebrow. "Is that so?" he murmured. "Well … I'll get one of the rifles out of the cabinet in the study, just in case. But if I'm hearing you correctly, then you are suggesting that should they come after us here, we … run?" He sounded like he was open to the suggestion.

"Yessir," Arch said, opening the door to the Explorer. "Get in the car and just go. You and the whole family." He frowned. "Is Brian here?" Brian was Alison's brother, just returned from getting a doctorate in philosophy from somewhere up north, somewhere Ivy League, though Arch couldn't remember quite where.

"He's in the basement," Longholt said with an amused air. "He won't be of much use in a fight, though."

"Didn't think he would be," Arch said. His brother-in-law was not the sort who had ever been in a fight in his life. "Still and all, you might want to warn him, let him know so he can get out with y'all."

"I shall apprise him," Mr. Longholt said with a faint smile. "I don't expect we'll be hearing much about this after the morning, though?"

Arch stared evenly at his father-in-law and suspected he had his answer for what the man had been trying to say earlier. "No. If everything goes right, I don't expect you will."

Chapter 11

Hendricks was sitting quietly in the hotel room when he heard the car pull up outside. He had his coat back on, sword and gun in his belt, and he was ready to give it hell. He opened the door and shut it quietly after checking on Erin one last time. He left her keys on the nightstand with a note explaining he'd gone out with Arch and that she'd passed out before they'd had a chance to do much of anything. He was hoping to make it back before she woke up, so he could explain it to her in person, but he didn't have much confidence that what he was heading off into could be wrapped up either easily or quickly.

"How's Erin?" Arch asked him as he stepped off the curb, heading for the passenger seat.

Hendricks didn't answer until he was strapping in. "She's fine. Probably gonna have a headache in the morning, for more than one reason." Hendricks lowered his voice, like he was talking about something indelicate. "How's your wife?"

Arch set his jaw as he backed the police car out of the space. "Quiet." They hit the highway and turned left, heading toward Kilner Road. There was a silence for about five minutes before Arch spoke again. "Where's that other woman? Starling?"

"Hell if I know."

*

Ygrusibas could feel the ancient power surging, swelling within now. It had taken a while, but it was here, the fury of the full strength of one of the old ones. The night was lit like day, the cow's eyes adapting to the new power flooding into the shell. The ability to make changes was soon at hand, was coming, and then … then Ygrusibas would be free.

Creampuff mooed and tried for a patch of grass but was swiftly rebuked and kept from moving. Such things were not befitting an ancient. Only flesh would suffice.

*

"Do you think they'll know we're coming for them?" Arch asked, letting a little of his uncertainty show to the quiet ex-Marine on the other side of the cruiser. It wasn't exactly his first raid, but he hadn't done many scenarios like this, other than at the academy, and especially after how things had gone earlier, it was a little nerve-racking. More than a little.

"They're dumb if they don't," Hendricks replied. That reassured Arch more than he would have thought. "Two of their kind got away from me, how many from the ones that attacked you?"

"None."

Hendricks stared at Arch, his eyebrow slightly raised. "How many did they send? One or two?"

"Four," Arch said, guiding the Explorer into a turn onto Kilner Road.

Hendricks made a choked noise. "You took out four demons? With the switchblade I gave you?"

Arch shook his head. "I think I got two of them with that?"

Hendricks was quiet for a second, waiting for an explanation. "How'd you kill the others?"

"Impaled one of them on a wall stud," Arch said, flipping his lights off and coasting down the gravel road by the moonlight shining down through the trees overhead. "Busted another one open with a broken sink."

"Jesus," Hendricks said, muted. "I've never even heard of anything like that."

Arch grunted. "Wouldn't have been my first choice for how to do it, that's for sure."

They lapsed into silence as Arch took the car over to the side of the road. "Approach from the same direction as last time or come at them from behind the house?"

Hendricks gave it a moment's thought. "Last time they caught us because those two guys were out getting high, right?" He waited for Arch's nod. "It stands to reason that they're not gonna be out getting high this time, since we killed them."

Arch nodded at that, but it didn't do much to soothe him. A question emerged in his mind. "How do demons get high if they're … y'know, not human?"

"Not really sure," Hendricks said, opening the door. "I know they're susceptible to a lot of the same things that humans use, though. Maybe all. Dependence is a pretty big issue in the demon community, I'm told. And you really don't want to see one of them on amphetamines, let me tell you that."

Arch nodded; even the humans he'd run across who were coked-up or on meth were a pain to put down. Adding strength to demons seemed like a formula for complete and utter disaster.

They made their way over the fence, careful again to dodge the electric wire. The crunch of leaves beneath their shoes was muted as they took their time, trying to keep an eye out all around them, in front, behind, and on both sides. Arch wore himself out keeping his head swiveling and nearly tripped over a fallen log when he thought he heard the sound of a car going by on Kilner Road.

"Might want to keep your eye on the trail," Hendricks said, muted enough that it was nearly lost under the whisper of the wind.

Arch just grunted low. They were almost to the treeline, and when they came out, they both crouched low and headed toward the top of the hill. The moon shone down on them, a few clouds visible in patches throughout the sky. The smell of the dairy farm was heavy in the air, a thick scent that didn't bother Arch at all. He caught Hendricks turning up his nose a couple times, though. "Aren't you from Wisconsin, the dairy state?" Arch asked in a low whisper.

"Yeah, but I didn't live on one of the farms," Hendricks replied. "I lived in town, like you."

The moon slipped behind one of the clouds as the wind picked up a little more and Arch felt it run cool over his skin. It always took until nearly midnight for things to feel remotely nice out in the summer. The faint noise of crickets in the distance caught his gaze, until something moved in the house below, and a porch light came on.

"Shit," Hendricks hissed. "I think they're coming out!"

"Hold on," Arch said, turning to see if they were by chance being flanked. He saw nothing behind them, no sign of anything. "I don't think they know we're here."

There was a noise of footsteps and faint barks of talking down below. The house was a good ways in the distance, a hundred yards or more, and the voices weren't clear. The figures on the MacGruders' porch were just silhouettes, two of them, and they were joined a moment later by five more, three of them clearly bound in some way. One of them screamed, loud and long, and Arch felt himself tense as the figure—clearly a woman from the scream—was hit in the face. "They have hostages," he said.

Hendricks's face was screwed up, watching the spectacle as the whole group started to move out toward the pasture gate, the demons in the rear bringing along the bound humans at a slow walk. "I don't think so. Prisoners, not hostages." Arch looked at the man, watched him as he chewed it over. "Sacrifices, I think."

Arch tried to puzzle through it, but he just didn't have enough information to even jump to a conclusion. "Sacrifices for what?"

Hendricks gave a little shrug. "Not sure. I never did hear back from my source on what ritual they might be performing, and my books aren't exactly comprehensive resources. All two of them."

Arch let his gaze follow the slow procession as the leading figure opened the gate to the far pasture. By his count there were four demons and three humans. "Any chance those sacrifices are actually demons, preparing an ambush for us?"

Hendricks answered almost immediately. "I doubt it but maybe. I guess if they wanted us to underestimate their numbers, go charging in like reckless idiots, that'd be one way to go about it. But I don't think so." A shriek cut through the night, and it sounded genuine. "No, I think this is it, unless they rounded up some more demons since they came after us earlier. Figure two survived their run-in with me, plus Hollywood and one more, a lackey for him, like a personal assistant, because he's the type of prima donna that would need one." Hendricks shook his head. "It's not a hundred percent, but I think this is genuine. We know they needed sacrifices, and it's damned near midnight, so I'm thinking we're about to see whatever ritual they're about to partake in."

Arch wanted to curse, but didn't. "And the sacrifices? They don't survive, I assume?"

"They're not called sacrifices for nothing," Hendricks replied.

"Let's go," Arch said, and they started to make their way down the hill as quietly as possible, trying to keep the dairy barn between them and the procession. It helped that the demons were speaking without bothering to be nearly as quiet as the two of them were.

*

Hollywood was ready. He was willing. It was time. Past time, actually, but that didn't really matter, so long as the sacrifices happened in the midnight hour. Last time he was probably too excited, maybe chanced it a little too close to the wire. Maybe killed them at eleven fifty-nine for all he knew. Whatever. That was then, it was a few takes back, now it was time to call *Action!* again and get on with the picture. And he was ready for his close-up, anyway.

He felt the familiar plop of his shoe hitting something he wished it hadn't but quelled the stream of profanities that came to mind. Why bother? The shoes weren't going to be important for much longer, anyway. Once Ygrusibas was called forth, was in his body, he'd be changed into another form, a glorious one. It was the ultimate power merger, really. A greater demon like Hollywood already had a body that was full to the brimming with essence, a tank that was to the top with awesome power. Add in an ancient like Ygrusibas, one of the first, one of the fallen, and the changes would be swift. Power would be a quaint notion he'd look back on as something cute, like a Chihuahua. He'd be a fucking Rottweiler. With an M-16.

"My book," he said, snapping his fingers at Sleeveless, who hustled up and opened it to the page that was already marked. Sleeveless was a good minion, better than the rest. It was a shame that he wasn't going to get much of a reward, but there were sacrifices that had to be made to bring about change, right? People suffered all the time, demons too. What was one more on the pile? It was just a plus one, that's all. A number.

Sleeveless held his cell phone, the face glowing, over the book so Hollywood could see. Good minion. He started to open his mouth to breathe the first words but another scream stopped him. He felt himself tense, irritated. He'd told Krauther to shut that bitch up—the whiny one, the teenager—but he clearly didn't have a very good handle on things.

Hollywood turned to give him a piece of his mind but stopped when he saw Krauther disappear into a blaze of hellfire, and the other nameless henchman followed a moment later.

*

Two down. That was Hendricks's thought as he and Arch took down Krauther and the spare, the ones who had been riding herd on the human sacrifices. He pushed the humans, bound, one of them gagged, behind him, he and Arch, making a little defensive line in front of them, positioning themselves between Hollywood and his intended sacrifices. The last demon was with Hollywood, cell phone clutched in his hand, the faceplate lit so Hollywood could read from his book. Hadn't these idiots ever heard of a flashlight?

"I'm glad you're here," Hollywood said, breaking the quiet that had persisted since Krauther had screamed like a bitch when Arch had ripped his back open and exposed his essence to the air. There was enough joy and amusement in Hollywood's voice that Hendricks thought he might actually be speaking genuinely. "I was worried we weren't going to have enough sacrifices, and it … I can't describe how galled I was that these idiots you killed failed to bring you back to me. Instead … you just show up on your own. It's like a gift from the heavens," Hollywood said with a wide grin that faded. "Speaking figuratively, of course. I don't get gifts from the heavens, and if I did, they'd probably be something I wouldn't care to open. Like a bag of flaming—"

"So they play that game in the underworld, too, huh?" Hendricks said, cutting Hollywood off. No point in listening to his blather. There was going to be a fight, the demon was probably a greater—which meant it was going to be ugly. Their best bet was to let Arch use the shotgun to put him down again while they both opened him up with swords. Save Munson—the guy with the cut-off flannel—for later, once Hollywood was safely ventilated. "Doesn't surprise me all that much that you'd be the one whose door they'd knock on for that."

"You guys really know how to step in it, you know that?" Hollywood laughed. "To continue the metaphor."

Hendricks couldn't see for sure, but he had a suspicion and went with it. "I don't think we're the ones who have stepped in it." Hollywood flushed; it was obvious in the moonlight. "So … we gonna rumble or do you just wanna keep running lines with us?"

Hollywood's smug look came back. "Oh, no, I'm about to call 'Action!' Just wanted to—"

"Monologue for a bit first?" Hendricks added in. "Like some cheeseball third-rate villain in a movie?"

Hollywood's smugness evaporated. "Haven't you heard? A desire to be understood is one of the most powerful motivations for any character." He smiled. "You don't know anything."

"I know a few things," Hendricks said, exchanging a look with Arch. "I know how to field strip and clean an M-16. I know Leinenkugel's is the best domestic beer ever made. I know the Green Bay Packers are the single greatest football team ever in American history." He pretended to think for a second. "Oh, and I know you don't like being shot in the face." He raised his .45 and fired off a double tap that nailed Hollywood right in the head both times.

Arch filled the air with a load of buckshot that echoed in Hendricks's ears as he blasted off a round at Munson. Hollywood staggered, stumbling back, and the book fell out of his hands to land on the ground. Hendricks crossed targets and shot Munson in the body once as he crossed the last few feet and landed his sword across the back of the demon's neck. He didn't get a chance to use his gun much when fighting because most of the places he fought were too populated, but he had to give Arch credit—shooting them first provided a welcome distraction. He ripped into Munson with the sword, opening up a gash as he hacked hard into where the spine would be on a human. Whether there was one in there was impossible to say; the wound welled up with orange light, and seconds later Munson was consumed in a scream of black flame, eaten from the inside by the fires of the netherworld taking him back.

Arch was already squaring up with Hollywood, firing his shotgun point blank in the demon's face. Hendricks wasn't sure, but he could swear he saw a little indentation from the buckshot as Hollywood's head snapped around, like it had landed but hadn't quite broken the skin. Close, maybe. If he lined up his shot and managed to shoot twice in roughly the same place …

There was an explosion of fury from the space where Hollywood was standing, and Hendricks felt it take him off his feet. His arms whirled as he flew a solid five feet off the ground into the air, and came to rest on the grassy earth, a jagged rock catching him in the right shoulder blade. Hendricks wanted to get up but was momentarily stunned; he tried to shake off the pain, and he wondered through the haze what the hell had just happened.

*

Arch had seen a little glow in Hollywood's eyes before he'd gone off, a little like a bomb. It wasn't hellfire coming out of him, though, more like a shockwave of force that sent Hendricks flying. Arch had been a little better braced, but it had still taken him off his feet. He'd been fortunate in his landing, shaking the feeling back into his brain real quick. Unfortunately, it hadn't been quickly enough to keep Hollywood from catching him around the neck and ripping the shotgun out of his grasp.

"You are so lucky this time," Hollywood said, pressing him to the ground. "See, this isn't a ten-thousand-dollar suit from London. You already ruined that, and I've made my peace with it. It's just a thing, you know, no big deal. Things aren't … important." There was an air of hesitancy in how he said it, like he was merely parroting the words. "Anyway, what's important is what comes next. And what comes next is history making. It's a new age." Hollywood was wearing a big grin. "The last age, really."

"Oh, yeah?" Arch tried to struggle off his knees, but Hollywood had him solidly. The switchblade was in Arch's pocket, and he was fumbling for it. This close, Arch could see a couple places where Hendricks had shot the demon, two spots on the forehead where there were slight creases, like something had pushed hard on a mask and made an indent. Arch still had the pistol on his belt, just had to bide his time for a minute, maybe, wait until Hollywood looked away. Hollywood was too fast and too watchful to try it now. Arch would end up separated from his body, likely as not, and that wasn't the way he wanted to go out.

"Yeah," Hollywood said and readjusted his grip to drag Arch across the pasture. Arch saw Hendricks, still writhing on the ground, as they swerved over to him. Hollywood aimed a hard kick at his guts. It made a heavy thump, like a watermelon being pounded in by a sledgehammer. and Hicks howled in pain. Arch wondered if the man had escaped internal injuries at that one, it had been so nasty.

"You three," Hollywood leveled a finger at the other people, the hostages, Arch still thought of them. With a start he realized it was the Blenkman family from just down the road. "You move, I will blur over to you and kill you without a single second's thought or remorse. Do you understand me? Nod if you understand. NOD, MOTHERFUCKERS!" The words crackled across the pasture and Arch saw them nod, even from the position Hollywood had squeezed him into, head down, locked into place with a hand at the base of his neck like he was a cat being manhandled by a farmer. "Okay, then," Hollywood said, picked up the book he'd dropped with his free hand, and hauled Arch up.

Hollywood stared at Arch for a minute, and Arch didn't really like the look of that. "Hey," the demon said at last. "I want you to know something before we get started. This thing," he pointed from himself to Arch, a dirty finger bobbing into Arch's face, "me killing you? It's not because you're black, okay? It's really important to me that you know that before we start."

Arch just stared at him. "I'm sure that will be of great consolation to my widow."

Hollywood looked at him blankly for a minute. "Well ... yeah, okay, that's a good point. But I really wanted you to know that, anyway, that it's not about race. I'm not a racist." He smiled a broad, almost apologetic smile. "Really. I'm totally down with the struggle. No, the reason I'm killing you is because you're on the side of the angels—and I'm most definitely not."

"Oh?" Arch felt a little of the feeling return in his fingers. "Side of the angels, huh? I haven't seen any of them show up to help me yet."

"And they won't," Hollywood said, adjusting himself so the book rested on his forearm, and opened to a pre-marked page with a cloth strip in place down the binding. "Because they don't get involved, not anymore. It was just a figure of speech." Hollywood looked up from his place in the book as the moonlight came down, illuminating the whole scene. "You are a righteous man, though. I can smell it on you," he turned his nose away, "like the stink of this cow pasture. You were just drawn into this, I bet, took to it like I took to producing, like it was the most natural thing in the world." He smiled as he leaned closer to Arch. "A lawman, a righteous man, and suddenly you find out there are demons walking the face of the earth? It was probably like you got awakened for the first time, like you'd finally found what you were called to do." Hollywood leaned in, the grin getting worse, the smell of something like sulfur on his breath. "I know your kind. I've met a few of yours, you incorruptible fucks, you self-righteous shits." He pushed Arch out to arm's length. "The nice thing about you is that your pure soul—I can just smell it from here—is gonna make a beautiful sacrifice—"

A low sound suddenly cracked around them, like thunder but louder than any thunder that Arch had ever heard. It was a rifle, he'd stake his life on it, and Hollywood was already staggering by the time they'd heard the sound, his arm severed from his body.

"Ohhh," Hollywood moaned, low and guttural, as he shuffled back. Arch staggered away from Hollywood, fingers still around his neck, but the hand disconnected from the demon at the shoulder. Arch ripped it away from him and threw it down, pulling his gun and aiming it at the disarmed Hollywood, who was still staggering around a few feet away, jerking like he'd been shocked instead of shot.

Arch backed up and made his way over to Hendricks, who was sitting upright now, his pistol back in one hand, sword in the other. "What the fuck did you do to him?" Hendricks asked.

"Nothing," Arch said. "Did you hear that gunshot?"

"That was a gunshot?" Hendricks said, his eyes a little glazed. "God, that must have been like a fifty cal or something. Big bore."

Arch shot a look back at Hollywood. "Something real big, I'd say, if it took his arm off." They both watched, waiting, as Hollywood jerked again, but seemed to steady himself on his feet. "Isn't he supposed to … you know, burn up now or get ripped back into the bowels of hell?"

"Doesn't work like that for greaters," Hendricks said and pulled up on Arch's arm to get back to his feet. "They don't just discorporate or disperse, whatever you want to call it. It's one of the reasons they're so dangerous."

"Because we're hard to kill," Hollywood said, looking at them, sounding like he was breathing hard. Arch wondered why he'd be breathing then figured it must all be part of the package that held them together.

"Pretty near impossible for you fleshy little fleas. You may have taken my arm—"

"We didn't take your arm," Arch said. Might as well get that out there. He wondered if there'd be another thunderous crack of the rifle in the distance and kind of hoped there would be. It'd be easier to figure out how to take the man down if someone would just blast his arms and legs off first. Not much threat from Hollywood if he was a quadruple amputee, lying on the ground. Arch would bet a decapitation would finish it then.

"Doesn't matter," Hollywood said, leering again. "You can't kill me. You can't stop me." There was a strange light over his features, like a glow being cast upon him. "I have come forth to end … your … world. Nothing of this earth can stop me—"

Hollywood stopped as the glow became lighter, like the sunrise in the distance. Except that was a good five or six hours away, by Arch's reckoning. There was something else, closer, just up the hill, like a lamp growing brighter, drawing closer to them as it came. It got to near blinding, and the wind picked up again and brought with it a smell of sulfur, of brimstone, and Arch had to cover his nose. Hendricks was leaning on him for support, and they both stood there, staring, caught between watching Hollywood and watching the new entrant, until the light finally died down.

It was a cow, Arch thought. Or had been. It was changed into something grotesque, standing on two legs, with swollen hooves and bifurcated legs that gave it balance. It stood twice the height of a man, and when it snorted, hellfire flared out of its nostrils along with a strong smell of sulfur. It had arms like a man, cloven fists, and a face that was positively frightening, with a keen intelligence that looked over all of them, down at the bottom of the hill. In two steps it was almost upon them. Arch heard the screams of the three Blenkmans behind him and he knew they were fleeing. He resisted the temptation to follow them. The thing standing in front of him was all manner of … just *wrong*.

He felt Hendricks tense at his side. "So that's what they were summoning."

There was a pause, and the cow-demon spoke, low and harsh, breathing fire out its nostrils as it did so. "I am Ygrusibas, the harbinger of end-times, the first sign of your world's end, the breath of the apocalypse."

Arch just stood there, next to Hendricks, fingers idly fiddling with the switchblade he'd pulled out of his pocket and the pistol he'd pulled with his other hand. Neither of them said anything, Arch trying to figure out what to do, whether to bum rush the thing or wait, and Hendricks probably running through just about the same thought. Nobody spoke for about a minute.

Finally it was Hollywood who said something. "You know what? Fuck this place."

Chapter 12

"Seriously," Hollywood said, just letting the rage run through him. "Fuck this town, fuck the South, you backwards hillbillies." He pointed a finger at Arch. "In L.A, a pure heart like yours gets eaten while it's still pumping blood. You're a nothing, there. Fodder for the fucking gristmill. You're an aperitif, swallowed and gone in an eyeblink." He turned to point his finger to Hendricks. "And you? What have you got? A hard-on for revenge? Some mystery backstory and score to settle? OOOOH!" Hollywood waved his remaining arm in mockery. "Vague and mysterious may have sold screenplays in the nineties, but you're played out, now. You're not even a problem I'd have to solve. You're a man on a suicide mission, and you'll just keep circling lower and lower until you crash all on your own. I know your kind. I can smell you a mile off just from the stink of your past failures, hanging around you like the cloud that hovers over this dump."

He wheeled on Ygrusibas, took in the whole distorted cow form, on the verge of becoming something glorious, though he really didn't want to admit that to himself. "And you? You blew it, motherfucker! I called you forth, I brought you out of your torment. You were supposed to reward me, to join with me—so we could go about the apocalypse together." He twisted two fingers together, trying to show this idiot ancient what partnership was all about. "I mean, really? A cow? Do you know who I am? I'm a fucking producer for fuck's sake!" He thumped his chest. "I ALMOST GOT A SCREENWRITING CREDIT ON BATTLESHIP, YOU MOTHERFUCKER!" He took a breath in through his nose then let it out through his mouth. "I'm a greater. A demon of the highest order, and you have seriously fucked up here—"

That was as far as he got. Ygrusibas dipped it's head, blazed in faster than Hollywood would have believed possible, even for an ancient, and there was a sound of cracking bones as he was swallowed nearly whole by the cow-demon, his essencc still howling with fury as he was dissolved into something more ancient and powerful than he.

*

"Holy shit," Hendricks said, not really sure what else to say. His whole body still ached from Hollywood's last attack, and his stomach was positively throbbing. "Did our unstoppable bad guy just get eaten by a cow?" Hollywood had been gobbled up in two big bites.

"Either that or we just got killed and this is heaven," Arch said, the strain evident in his voice.

"This is your idea of heaven?" Hendricks asked, not taking his eyes off the cow-demon. "Watching someone you dislike get swallowed whole by a bovine hellspawn? You religious people are even more fucked up than I always thought."

"Your world will end," Ygrusibas said and came snapping at them. The only thing that gave them enough time to dodge was the crack of another rifle shot. Ygrusibas staggered back, and Hendricks saw a hole in the demon's arm burning with internal fire.

*

Arch ran to the side as a burst of flame lit the night, turning it almost into day, at least around their little corner of the pasture. It made him reconsider that thought about him being in heaven. Fire was more likely to indicate the other place.

Another crack thundered through the night and Arch saw the cow-demon stop again and roar, flames filling the air above them. "Who the hell is firing off that rifle?" Hendricks shouted, popping off three rounds from his .45.

"I don't know," Arch said, pulling the trigger of his Glock, aiming for the demon's eyes. "But I reckon we owe them our gratitude, don't we?" He figured the rifle was the only thing keeping the cow-demon from rolling right over them and being on after the next part of its business. Since it had mentioned ending the world, this was of more than a little concern to Arch.

He hadn't met many demons, but if this was what they were all up to and about, it seemed like he might have been backing the right side all along. He fired again then scrambled as Ygrusibas charged at him, head lowered. Even the rifle crack didn't stop him this time.

*

Hendricks heard Arch howl as Ygrusibas picked him up after nearly running him down. Hendricks kept firing his pistol, but he heard it go click after a couple more shots. Arch was suspended by his ankle, flailing a little. Desperate, Hendricks just up and threw the pistol to hit Ygrusibas in the head with it. He didn't have any spare mags on him, anyway.

Hendricks charged at the creature's leg and stabbed, hard, into the knee with the sword. He opened a gash and saw a burst of orange light, more fire than he could ever recall seeing, like it was actually bleeding out, and it got damned hot all the sudden. He yanked the sword back. Flames licked out of the wound he'd made, burning him. Something grabbed him firmly around the ankle, and he was swept off his feet, his hat falling off his head and his coat hanging down around his shoulders.

He hung onto his sword, though.

*

Ygrusibas hadn't seen these things before, these humans, these petty beasts. He knew of them, knew of the trouble they'd brought, had heard the whispers in the pits, but it was all idle chatter until now. They were weak, nearly empty of essence, empty of any meaning. He looked at the two in his grasp, staring from one back to the other. He wondered how any such thing, so small, so tiny, could cause such problems—

There was a searing pain in his hand, and he shook the one wearing black until the sparkling sword fell from his grasp. Such a small thing to cause such pain. There was a crack of noise again and another sting. This, though, was an even smaller worry than these two, these curiosities. Only a moment's more examination and he would feed on them, take the little sustenance their essences offered, and be on his way. This whole world, if it was filled with these things, would offer only the slightest distraction for

Ygrusibas. Ygrusibas was a consumer, would eat it all, would grow more powerful with the feeding, the dissolving of the essences within him. He was powerful enough now to anchor himself here, as a hedge against ever being drawn back to the pits.

He narrowed his eyes and looked once more at the figures in his hands. Trifles, that was all they were. Nothing compared to the greater demon he'd just consumed. But they were more than the herd of cows he'd had before, and that was something.

*

Another rifle crack sounded like desperation to Arch, like whoever was at the trigger of the thing knew it wasn't doing much good. Ygrusibas took less notice of it than he had any of the prior shots, and Arch was getting a real good close up of the cow-demon's eye when the latest shot rang out. The thing didn't even blink in its study of him.

"Any ideas?" he shouted to Hendricks. The cowboy wasn't moving, not right now, anyway. Between Hollywood and Ygrusibas, Arch reckoned he'd had a rough night, his arms limp and his sword dropped after he'd been shaken for stabbing the cow-demon. The sword had opened a thin line of fire along the hairy knuckle. Arch was still half-expecting blood to come rushing out, but it didn't. Just that same hellfire that had seeped from the stump of Hollywood's arm. "Come on, cowboy!" Arch said. "Look at this thing. You should be riding herd on it!" He estimated he was about ten seconds from being gobbled up. Whenever this thing got done peering at him, he was pretty well finished, and that wasn't going to do for him. He had things to say to Alison. He hadn't left it off very well, he knew that, but he'd thought somewhat stupidly that he was walking into something less hazardous than the fight he'd waltzed into.

A movement behind Ygrusibas's leg caught Arch's attention. He thought at first it was one of the Blenkmans coming back. It took him a minute to realize it was a red-haired woman, strolling somewhat casually up behind the cow-demon. He watched, waiting, as the grip on his leg grew tighter and he felt the end coming up fast.

*

Hendricks awoke to a sort of vague shout from Arch, something about cowboys and riding herd. He was aching all over, ribs, sternum, even his leg where the demon held him. His head was spinning, probably from being suspended upside down, but there wasn't in a position to do about that. No gun, no sword. He might as well have taken out his dick and tried slapping Ygrusibas with that for all the effect it would have.

He blinked and realized there was someone moving behind the cow-demon, someone with red hair who wore black. He wanted to believe it was real, but the potential for a hallucination crossed his mind. He started to say something but the figure grew clearer. It was Starling, no doubt, and she was standing just between the demon's legs. "Uh …" he called out to her, quietly, but enough that he saw a flash of red hair as she turned toward him, "… a little help here?"

Starling stared at him, and he felt for a moment that a current of electricity snapped between them. Then he thought it might just have been the cumulative effect of the beatings he'd suffered. Either way, she was looking at him, looking, then moving—

Ygrusibas screamed, a cry loud enough to rend the air itself, like Hollywood's shock wave all over again but sonic this time. Hendricks's skull hurt, but not just from the sound, he realized after a moment. It was because he'd been dropped on his head.

*

Arch was waiting for it, hoping for it. For a flash he'd thought maybe Starling had been working with Ygrusibas all along, some kind of feint and betrayal, but she'd stood beneath the demon's legs, reached out, and ripped the calves of the thing clean off. It had dropped him in a hot second, Hendricks too. Arch had managed to catch himself before he hit the ground, landing on his knees in the soft grass. Hendricks didn't look to be quite so lucky.

Arch was scrambling a second later. Instinct told him that this wasn't going to last, that whatever Starling had done was just temporary. Ygrusibas was flat on its back, and Arch still had the switchblade in his hand. He clambered onto the cow-demon's massive torso like a cat climbing a human, and he started digging in with the knife, dragging it between ribs as he kept moving.

*

It took Hendricks a moment to realize that the screams weren't his. He was hazy, really hazy, maybe worse than the time in Iraq when a mortar had gone off way too close to him. This wasn't Iraq, though, it was a cow pasture, and he was fighting a demon. Or had been. Now he was fighting a cow that had eaten a demon. Actually he was sitting back watching it happen, but that took another moment for him to figure out.

Arch was clawing the thing across the extra-sized ribcage. He was making some decent headway, too, if the lines of fire that were crisscrossing its torso were any indication. Hendricks searched for his sword and found it nearby. He picked it up and went to join Arch—maybe see if he could cause some screaming of his own.

*

Whatever Starling had done had put Ygrusibas down hard. Arch might have been more impressed if he'd had time to think about it. As it was, he was trying to keep the cow-demon from ending him, and the only advantage he had was that it was still seemingly disabled by Starling's efforts. Where had she gone? He made a mental note to look for her later, maybe say thanks somehow. If they made it out of this.

Hendricks was right there with him in a second. He started hacking at the thing with the sword, and it was starting to look like a little pyre, like someone had set a fire under Ygrusibas. It was bleeding out through the rips and tears in the cowhide. He almost got a laugh out of that. It looked no more like leather in its current state than chicken crap looked like chicken salad.

*

Hendricks stabbed deep into Ygrusibas's chest, and his sword clacked on thick bones on either side of the wound. No blood came out, just more of the heat, more of the fire, something that made him want to recoil. He didn't though, not much. The pains on his body were dull, but he squinted into the mess he'd created. The heart should be in there, he would have thought. He couldn't see it, though, just a bright light somewhere in the center of the body of the beast, a surging fire that was so hot he would swear he was about to burst into flames himself.

*

Arch saw it through the openings he'd made in Ygrusibas—Hendricks's blade, deep inside. The smell of brimstone was everywhere, but for some reason he didn't even have to look away from the burning flames, couldn't feel any heat from them. If anything, they were cold to him. He reached past them, stabbing deeper with the switchblade, aiming for the blazing center of the demon, the heart. He tapped the light within, just tapped it, his arm buried way past the elbow. There was a flash, and suddenly he was tumbling down.

*

The burst of heat that followed Arch's stab to the light was incredible. Hendricks hadn't ever done anything like this, but he had a suspicion he knew what was coming next. Even before Arch had reached his hand in—Hendricks wondering all the while how he wasn't burning up doing it—Hendricks was already pulling his sword out, dragging himself along, coat trailing behind him as he limped over to where Arch was half hanging out of the entrails of Ygrusibas. As soon as he saw the flash, like a bomb going off, he grabbed Arch by the legs and yanked him as hard as he could.

*

It was impossible. Ygrusibas could feel the heat within, the essences breaking free. There really weren't many of them, just the little ones from Creampuff and her brethren, the one from the greater demon he'd eaten, and then his own essence. It was considerable. It was formidable. It had taken HIM to imprison Ygrusibas, to cast him down. Now he was being brought down by these mites, these fleas. And her, the one who had brought him low. Who was she? He had caught a hint, only a hint, yet that was enough to torment him as the essences broke free and exploded around him.

The last thought Ygrusibas was left with was that she had been the one to beat him, really, not the fleas. Well, that and one last thought from somewhere deep within.

Moo.

*

Arch landed on top of Hendricks and heard the air rush out of the cowboy. They were both sprawled out, gasping, on the ground in the pasture, staring up at the moon above. It was the only light left now that the fire had dissipated. Arch was okay with that. Really okay with it.

It only took him a moment to sit up, to look over the whole situation. Hendricks was moaning, disgruntled and probably in more than a little pain. Starling stood a little farther away, staring down at both of them, still wearing that cold expression. He tried to decide what she was going to say before she said it.

*

"You are not seriously injured."

Hendricks would have been more enthused to hear Starling say that if he hadn't been still feeling the residual aches from the ass-kicking of a lifetime.

"You don't know that for sure," he replied, and tenderly pushed at his own abdomen. It felt a little achy but nothing screamed at him. Surprisingly. That Hollywood bastard had given him one hell of a kick to the gut. "Okay," he said after a pause. "Help me up?"

He felt strong hands assist him in getting to his feet. It took him a second to realize they were Starling's, not Arch's. He looked left to the deputy. "Pretty sure this lady just saved our lives."

Arch looked fairly neutral about it then turned to Starling. "Pretty sure he's right. Thank you kindly."

Starling looked from one of them to the other, almost curious, as though she were observing some strange phenomenon. She started to speak then stopped.

"Cat got your tongue?" Hendricks asked, almost smiling. Not quite, though. He was still hurting.

"No," Starling said.

Hendricks looked over at Arch and smiled. "I guess she doesn't know what to say to that."

Arch apparently didn't know what to say to that, either. And when Hendricks looked back at Starling to see what she had to say, she was gone.

*

"That was a hell of a thing," Hendricks said as they limped toward the road. Arch had handed him his gun and his sword, and they were on their way out now, Hendricks moving under his own power, but slowly. Arch was a foot or so to his side, shotgun over his shoulder.

"Yeah, I don't reckon I've seen anything quite like it before," Arch said.

"Neither have I," Hendricks agreed. "Five years I've been doing this, never squared off against a greater, let alone seen one get eaten by the cow-demon he summoned himself." He smiled because damn if it wasn't funny. "Seems like there's some irony in that. What's that old phrase? 'Hoist on your own petard'?"

"Hollywood got hoisted, all right," Arch said.

The night had gotten quiet, and they walked along in silence for a spell, until Arch spoke again.

"So, you gonna head out of town now?" Arch asked. He phrased it like a serious question, and Hendricks pretended to think it over.

"Right now I'm gonna drag ass back to my motel room and pass out," Hendricks said. "But no, I'm not planning to leave just yet. Unless this was the cause of the hotspot." He chucked a thumb over his shoulder to indicate all that, the shit they'd just tromped through. "Then I suppose I'd clear out, head on to the next."

Arch pondered it, not saying nothing for a sec. "Is that likely?"

This was a serious question. "Hell if I know," Hendricks said. "I don't know what starts 'em, I don't know what causes 'em to die off. Hell, I don't even know what the allure is, what makes these things such a draw for the hellfire and brimstone crowd. I just know that where one pipes up, they show up in droves." He felt serious now, and the pain was a secondary consideration for just a minute. "Wherever they go, I'll be there, too." He wondered if Arch would ask and was not too disappointed when he did.

"What'd they do to you?" Arch looked sidelong at Hendricks, and Hendricks just kept walking, trying to decide how to answer.

"They took everything from me," he finally said. And really, that pretty much covered it. They walked on in silence.

Chapter 13

Arch dropped Hendricks off at the motel sometime later, after a quiet ride back. There wasn't much left to say, for the moment, at least. Hendricks hadn't answered, not in any meaningful way. What was everything to one man was another man's tackle box or hunting rifle or Harley. It made Arch curious, but not achingly so. If the cowboy didn't want to answer, he didn't have to, and Arch just watched him walk back up to the motel room door after they'd shaken hands without a word exchanged. They didn't have to say anything. Not right now, anyway.

*

Hendricks listened to the quiet creak of the door as he opened then shut it carefully, trying not to disturb the figure that was still lying on the bed. It didn't work, though, and she moved as soon as the beam of light from the open door disappeared. He could see her move in the dark, sitting up by the faint light making its way in from the motel sign outside. It shone in around the edges of the curtains, casting the whole place with a shadowed look. Another room in another town. The girl in his bed was new, though.

"Hey," she said in a sleepy voice.

"Hey," he said, and glided over to the chair. He took off his hat and coat, taking care to hide the sword in the depths of the drover before he removed it. The gun went safely into the inside pocket as well, before he balled the whole mess up and let it lie on the floor. His next stop was the edge of the bed. "How are you feeling?"

"Little headache," she said, and he could see her soft features as his eyes adjusted. She looked down. "I'm still wearing my clothes and you're just getting back here at two A.M. so I'm guessing we didn't …" She just let it trail off, and he waited to see if she'd finish the thought.

"No, we didn't," he answered after a pause. "You passed out and hit your head, and then Arch called, so I went with him to deal with some … stuff." He realized how lame that sounded to even his ears. He didn't really want to think too deeply about what it must sound like to her.

"Oh." She didn't sound too mad, fortunately. "So we didn't fuck?" He shook his head slowly. "Did I at least blow you?" He kept shaking it. She laughed, but it sounded a little hoarse, like her throat was scratchy. "God, am I a buzzkill or what? Just passed out on you after all that making out?"

"Clearly you weren't feeling too well," Hendricks said, with a little remorse over lying to her like this. It was still better than telling her a demon had smacked her head against the wall and he'd had to light out to stop it from ending the world. Though, if he'd thought she would have believed it, he would have gone with that. It made him sound way cooler. "We might have overdone it a little with all those beers."

"Like I'm some kind of lightweight?" She was amused, but there was a challenge there. She didn't sound sleepy anymore. Her hand snaked out and was on his side, up his shirt, and she didn't notice him cringe in the dark as she hit a bruised spot. "Listen, cowboy, I can outdrink you anytime, and still have enough energy to ride you all night long even after you've passed out."

"Is that so?" It wasn't in his nature to be challenging with a woman, but in this case, it felt like the right thing to say.

"You're damned right it is."

She was on him after that, her mouth on his, that pressure building again under all his myriad aches and pains. She was a little rougher than he expected, struggling to get his shirt off. Hers came off fast, just a few buttons and it was over her head. He remembered where the clasp for her bra was, and it came off quickly, too.

"I got into a car accident last week," he said, holding her hands to keep her from twisting him out of his shirt. "Still really bruised up, so take it easy." She didn't acknowledge him verbally, but she nodded, and she was gentler taking his shirt off. If her eyes widened at the sight of the bandages still covering his chest, he couldn't see it in the dark.

He eased her pants off, her panties too, and found her almost as ready as he'd left her a few hours earlier. That was a good thing, he figured, a woman who warmed up easily. Beat the hell out of the alternative, especially for a late-night roll in the hay. His mouth ran across her nipples while his hand worked her clit. She was grasping for him as well, trying to get a hand on his cock. He kept her from it, though, long enough for him to come back up to her, to kiss her lips, and by then she was moaning for him to get on with it.

He slipped into her with feverish desire, still sweating from the heat of the fight. He started slowly, building with intensity as the minutes rolled on. She moaned her agreement. Her hands went by turns delicately caressing his chest, then running down his shoulders, and finally grasping at his ass and pulling him in deeper. She held him there until he thrust one last time and she gasped, letting out an exhalation before she went slack.

It took him just a little longer to reach his own climax, but when he did he slumped on her, leaving himself inside her. He buried his face in her neck, in the scent of her sweat mixed with the perfume she'd worn. She felt sticky from top to bottom, every part of him in contact with her, nothing between them at all, and Hendricks began to feel more exposed than he'd felt in a long, long time.

*

Arch stayed out in the driveway of his in-laws house for about five minutes before the front porch light came on. He hadn't wanted to wake anyone and had reconciled himself to sleeping in the car. The minute he saw the light come on, though, he was out of the cruiser and on his way up. He had a fresh magazine in the Glock and a round was chambered. He kept a hand on that, and the other deep in the pocket where the switchblade rested. He wondered when Hendricks would need it back, and how he'd ever feel safe without carrying it all the time.

Alison was at the door, silhouetted with her blond hair all loose around her head. Arch wanted to run to her, but he calmed himself. He was a man, a man of the old school, and he didn't go in for big displays of emotion one way or another. The fact that he knew that about himself was a measure of him in a way, but not one he liked to think about overly much. Introspection wasn't his thing, and walking up to his in-laws porch wasn't the place for it anyway, not with things as they were.

"Hey," Alison said and folded him into her arms before he had a chance to say anything.

"Hey, babe," he replied and hugged her back. He held her tight for a moment without speaking. "About last night—"

"We don't need to talk about it anymore," she said and stepped back, but took his hand in hers.

That one threw him back for a spell. She always wanted to talk. About everything. "Are you sure?"

Her eyes were flat, unflinching. She may have just been tired, but it felt like they were muted somehow. "You took care of it, didn't you?"

It took him a moment to realize that the proverbial "it" could have been any number of things, all rolled up into one. He thought about explaining it, maybe giving her some detail or saying something reassuring. Finally, he just nodded.

"Then come to bed," Alison said, and he followed her inside. They shut the door, and she led him off, down the hall to her old room, and they went inside and turned off the light.

*

Hendricks woke early, Erin draped across his body. He woke up kind of natural, with a hard-on still pressed into her hip where she was laying on him. He grinned even though it felt a little awkward, not really sure how to extract himself from this situation and even less sure he wanted to. Although his chest kind of hurt with her on it, it wasn't bad enough to make him want to wake up the sleeping little angel who was stirring his chest hair with her every breath.

"What are you so tickled about?" she asked him in a voice that carried not even a hint of sleepiness. When he looked down, her eyes were still pressed tightly closed, but she had a faint smile on her face. "Are you laughing about poking me awake?" The eyes came open now, and they were alight with mirth, perfectly matching the smile.

"Nah," Hendricks said, then jabbed her again, eliciting a giggle from her. "Just nice to have someone here besides myself to deal with it ..."

After they'd dealt with it, they showered together, with that surprising shyness that comes with a morning after. Hendricks plunged right through it, kissing her frequently, as much to remind himself of what he'd done with her, to feel the new sensations it brought with it, as to assuage the burgeoning sense of guilt he felt. Like a betrayal of things long past. She didn't ask him about it, and he hoped it didn't show. Still, he kissed her and held her in the shower more than he needed to. Overcompensating, maybe. He threw himself into it with as much enthusiasm as he could, pushing away that nagging sense of doubt, of being out of place and uncomfortable.

She dressed when they'd finished, putting on her uniform again. "Where are my panties?" she asked, searching the bed sheets. He watched her from afar, brushing his teeth at the sink. "Have you seen them?"

"Not sure," he replied, taking the toothbrush out of his mouth. He was trying to spit quietly, unobtrusively, not wanting to draw any attention to himself. Like he hadn't just stared at her naked body for the last several hours, in darkness and light. And he was embarrassed about brushing his teeth and spitting in front of her. She'd had his dick in her mouth less than an hour ago and his face had been buried between her legs, but he felt a blush at making a noise to get the paste out of his mouth. For chrissakes. "Want a pair of my boxers?"

She turned and studied him in the mirror. "Guess they'll have to do, because I have no idea where my panties went. My belt can probably keep them up, right?" She came up behind him as he wordlessly handed her a pair of plaid boxer shorts. "Say, you're not one of those guys that keeps panties as a trophy of his conquests, are you?" He wordlessly shook his head, trying not to spit until she walked away. "Good. I dated one of those creepers once."

He delicately got rid of the toothpaste and took a drink from the faucet from one of the motel's cups. "I'll see if I can find them later, once housekeeping takes a stab at this place. They probably just got lost in the …" He took her in his arms as she began to button her uniform top. She looked cute, bra partially exposed, wearing his boxers, tanned legs with no pants. It was an abstract sort of interest, though. He knew he didn't have it in him to go again, not this morning. Besides, he was legitimately in pain now. "Well, you know. Anyway, I'll look once the place gets cleaned up a bit."

"I guess I'll just borrow these for a while," Erin said with a half-smile as she pulled away from him and retrieved her pants, then started to slide them up while he watched the boxers disappear under her khaki uniform bottoms.

"Seems only fair," Hendricks said, deciding now was as good a time as any to drop a shoe on her. "I did borrow your car last night, after all."

"*What?*"

*

Arch walked into the sheriff's station just before seven and caught a sympathetic smile from Erin, who was already sitting at the front desk. He looked briefly but couldn't see any sign of where she'd hit her head. Her hair looked clean, but different, like she'd braided it back for some reason. He didn't put too much more thought into it because Nicholas Reeve popped his head out of his office just then and waved Arch back. Arch did as he was bid.

He stepped into Reeve's office, the dark wood paneling a leftover from the last major renovation of the sheriff's station. Reeve had an old-fashioned gun cabinet in the corner of the room, filled to the brim with rifles. Those were pretty common in Calhoun County, though. His father in-law had one almost exactly like it for all his guns. It wasn't exactly the last word in safety, but it was a nice feature for a lawman's office to have. It certainly looked more presentable than modern gun safes, with their scoured metal surfaces.

"So," Reeve said once they were both settled. "You want me to have Erin get you some coffee?"

"I'm fine," Arch said, settling into the padding of the seat. He was only as loose as he was because he was tired. Otherwise he'd have been about as bristly as a cat running over a floor of electrified chicken wire.

"Is that your usual stoicism?" Reeve asked, putting his hands back behind his head. "Or are you calmed down because the situation has been dealt with?"

Arch had spent the second half of the night trying to figure out what to say here. It really hinged on one thing—how much leeway Reeve was going to be willing to give him. "What have you heard?" he asked.

"Well," Reeve started, drawling a little, "I've got the members of the Blenkman family—you know them, MacGruder's neighbors—saying that Bric Munson and another couple of his ilk came over to their house and broke in, took them hostage. Said it was some sort of Satanic ritual, that the guys were all drugged out on something." Reeve watched him carefully, and Arch knew he was being watched. It wasn't even a game between them now; Reeve was just going to say what he needed to say. "It's a funny thing. They claim they saw some scary stuff, but that some guy in a cowboy hat and our old football hero Arch Stan saved their lives." He wasn't giving much away about his own thoughts, just sticking with the story. "Course they got scared and ran home after seeing what they described as," he picked up a witness report on a standard form that was lying on his desk and read from it, "the biggest man any of them had ever seen, armed with a flamethrower." He set it back down and a kind of skepticism came over him. "You believe that shit?"

"I believe what I saw," Arch said. "And there was a whole lot of flame flying around, I reckon."

Reeve puckered his lips, twisting them in contemplation. "Uh huh. I take it MacGruder's dead?"

Arch didn't hesitate on that one. "I think it's a safe bet Munson and his boys killed him and his wife, yes. Though there wasn't much sign of them from what I saw."

Reeve gave that a moment of thought. "Too many ways to make a body disappear in Calhoun County. Throw 'em in the Caledonia River, bury 'em in the woods, throw 'em in one of the mine shafts up on Mount Horeb, or down in a cave." He shook his head. "Lots of ways to get rid of bodies 'round here." He looked back at Arch. "Do you suppose we'll ever find these boys that broke into your house, attacked your pretty young wife?"

Arch could tell he was being tested, and he wasn't sure what the right answer was in Reeve's mind, not for a certainty. But there was the honest answer, and he went with it. "No, sir. I don't suspect we'll ever find them, not at all."

Reeve just gave a slow nod as he leaned back in his chair. "Good. I reckon things are better that way."

*

Arch caught up with Hendricks about midday at the diner out by the interstate. Even deputies had to eat, and if his path took him past the place where he suspected Hendricks would have to show his face sooner or later, and it happened to be close to the interstate, where he could fill the county's coffers by writing tickets on speeding out-of-towners, well, it was all the better so far as the sheriff would be concerned. Though Arch suspected he wouldn't ask about that. He suspected he wouldn't ask about much of anything, now, after their conversation this morning. He had a sense of Reeve that he hadn't had before, and he could only describe it as something he would have found deeply disquieting only a few days earlier. Now he was trying to muster any outrage at all and failing.

"How do," Hendricks said as Arch slid in across from him. The diner crowd was buzzing a little. Thursday at noon, a few of the locals were hanging around. Plenty of interstate traffic to go along with that, too.

"Making it just fine," Arch said as he held up a finger to the waitress from across the room.

Hendricks watched. "So, is this a thing with you? You just hold up a finger in whatever establishment you go to, and they just bring you whatever's popular, even if they don't know you?"

"They know me here," Arch said. "I come in for lunch at least three times a week. Always order the same thing, too."

"Oh, yeah?" Hendricks nodded his head. "You didn't talk to Erin, did you?"

"No," Arch said. Light was shining in through the big plate glass window to his left, and a pickup truck cruising by caught the glare. "Why?"

Hendricks gave a half-smile. "She was okay with getting falling down drunk and getting hit in the head, but I think I made her mad when I told her I borrowed her car."

Arch raised an eyebrow at him. "That's grand theft auto."

"Your life was in the balance." Hendricks took a bite of a fry. There was no ketchup anywhere on his plate.

"Well, in that case," Arch said, "all is forgiven."

Hendricks was watching him, looking for irony. "Really?"

"On my end it is, but I'm not the one who'd be pressing charges," Arch said. He looked around, to see if anyone was taking any interest in their talk. There was no booth behind him, and the one at Hendricks's back had a retiree from the paper mill that Arch knew. Man was deaf as a post. "The sheriff swept everything under the rug because he thinks I had some vendetta with Munson and Krauther. Those sacrifices told him we saved them, and he was already inclined to look the other way if I ran them to ground." He paused. "Literally to ground, in this case. Or six feet under it."

Hendricks stopped chewing. "He thinks you killed them?"

Arch looked around once more. "Yeah. Doesn't seem too bothered by it, either."

Hendricks started chewing again, but more delicately this time. "Questions abound about that. Is it because he's loyal, or because he knows what type of scum those guys were, or—"

"Or, or, or," Arch said, cutting him off. "Could be any, or all, or some other reason buried deep in the man's soul. No way to tell, really, at least not without having a conversation with the man that I don't want to have."

"Huh," Hendricks said. "Guess that works out for you, though."

"I'm not complaining," Arch said. Though he was finding it hard not to. "So you're hanging around for a while longer?"

"Not sure quite yet," Hendricks said, taking a look out the window as a Mack truck went by, heading to the truck stop just across the interstate. "I'm waiting for things to settle a little more, to get a read. Not sure if it's time for me to ride the wind on outta here yet."

Arch nodded, reading all that as pure poetry rather than literal truth. "What do you suppose happened to your girl Starling?"

Hendricks tightened up at that. Arch would have found it amusing, but he was a little too worn out for humor. "She's not my girl," he said. "And if you talk to Erin about her, please mention that she's your friend."

Arch gave a slight incline of his head. "She really saved the day last night. Saved the night, I guess. Anyway, I'd have no problem calling her a friend after that, at least until she shows me differently."

"That's good," Hendricks said. "You go with that, if Erin asks. If she wasn't happy about me borrowing her car, I can't imagine she'll be too happy with me having another woman driving it."

Arch stared back at Hendricks. "Is Erin just another girl to you?"

Hendricks gave it a moment's thought. "No. Why?"

"Just curious." A burger was set in front of Arch by the waitress just then, a big old plate of fries with them, and he grabbed the ketchup and started to tap the bottom of the bottle to get it out on his plate. "Wouldn't want to see her get hurt, that's all."

"I'm not aiming to hurt her," Hendricks said, watching Arch make a pile of red on his plate. The first fry always tasted the best, with the tang of the ketchup, the salt. Bliss. "Doesn't always stop it from happening, but it's not my intent."

"Good," Arch said, picking up his burger. "I'm gonna keep your knife for a while longer. Call it evidence seizure, if you have to."

"That's fine," Hendricks said, dabbing at his mouth with a napkin. "I think I feel better with you holding it than letting it sit in my hat. At least while this place is a hotspot." He looked around and gave a vague smile. "Normally, when a place goes hotspot, it's crawling with demons and demons hunters within days." His eyes walked around the room. "Half the people in this place would be familiar faces to me, people I'd run across down the trail." His eyes came back to Arch's, and the cowboy hat dipped to hide them. "I don't know any of these folks."

Arch looked around once. "Most are locals. Others look like interstate travelers, some truckers, maybe." He stared at the brim of Hendricks's cowboy hat. "Ain't no one dressed like you, that's for sure."

The faint smile came back to Hendricks's face, but it was mighty grim. "This isn't good. Demons are still coming into town. I caught signs of more of them migrating when I walked across the overpass this morning. Residual traces of sulfur smell, brimstone. They're coming, and the hunters aren't. This place, near as I can tell, is last in line."

"But you're here." Arch set his burger down. He didn't like where this was going.

"Me and me alone," Hendricks said. "But that's the rub. Like I said, this place oughta be crawling with hunters, but they're not showing and the demons are coming all the same."

Arch thought back, back to when they'd first met. "Didn't you tell me that some hotspots are just … destroyed? Burnt out cinders on a map when they're done?"

"I did indeed." Hendricks wasn't looking too coy right now. He didn't look sick, either, exactly, but to Arch he didn't seem far off. "So now you see the problem. Demons rolling into town, and we're a bit scarce on demon hunters. Because they keep trouble in check, and one guy," he pointed to himself, "all due respect to me and my mad skills, I can't keep watch on this whole town. Not by myself. And I damned sure can't handle an army of them alone."

Arch felt down in his pocket for the switchblade. It was still there and reassuring that it was. "Not alone." He looked out the window, at the dusty highway, the green hills and mountains of Tennessee beyond. Wondered how many of them were out there, hiding out, all across Calhoun County. "I'm gonna need a sword."

Hendricks smiled. "I might be able to help with that."

*

He shouldn't have been happy to have a partner of sorts, but he was. For a man who'd worked his ass off to spend the last five years isolated and alone, it was a strange sort of relief to Hendricks when Arch had bought in so quickly. A sword wouldn't be too much of a problem. She'd probably be glad to have another demon hunter on the team, even if it was just for as long as the hotspot lasted.

His room's phone was ringing when Hendricks got back to the motel. He answered it and heard the familiar buzz at the other end of the line, the low sound of something crackling. Regardless of when she called, or where she caught him, it was always there, ever present. He thought of it as the sound of power. He' figured that probably wasn't far off. "Hey. It's me."

"Ygrusibas was called forth, wasn't he?" Her voice was light, melodic. It didn't match her look, not at all, but he was almost relieved he didn't have to see her, not now. The shades were still pulled in the motel room and as he sat there on the edge of the bed, in the dark, he found he couldn't picture her. Which was probably just as well.

"He was," Hendricks said. They didn't need to exchange names. Never had. She knew who he was, and he knew her. Had since the day they'd met five years ago. "We put a halt to it."

There was a quiet, a pause. "You and Archibald Stan." There was something ominous about the way she said it.

"Yes. But he goes by Arch." He felt a bead of sweat roll down his face, and he knew it wasn't just the heat.

There was another pause, this one longer. "You need to stay there."

"The hotspot's still going, then?" Hendricks asked. Not that he expected a full and complete response, but sometimes he'd pan out a nugget or two in the search, things he wasn't expecting. Half the fun of a conversation with her was trying to get one of those, anyway. He had a suspicion that this time that the luck probably wasn't going to go his way. She'd already used Arch's name, after all. That was pretty abnormal since she never talked about anyone else but him and whatever demon he might be hunting.

"It will continue from here on out," she said. "All the way until the end."

Hendricks listened, waiting for more. When nothing else came, he asked. "The end of the world?" He felt a heavy sort of dread in his voice, which was surprising for a man who'd been living on borrowed time for so long.

"Yes." The answer was simple, understated. Just like everything she said.

Hendricks tried to figure out the best way to approach it, to say what he meant, and he finally just came out with it. "When's it going to start?"

The soft, melodic tone drifted from note to note in her answer. "It has already begun. It began with the rise of Ygrusibas and will march ever on from here until it reaches the hellish conclusion."

He blanched, even though she was handing out nuggets left and right at the moment. It was almost like he didn't want to hear any more. Didn't stop him from listening on anyway, though.

"Is there any way to stop it?" Hendricks asked. He thought about Erin. About Arch. "Any way at all?"

"There are possibilities," the voice returned. "But they remain only that, so long as Archibald Stan remains alive."

Hendricks sat up on the bed, ramrod, like something had been jabbed into his back. "What? So long as Arch remains alive? What the fuck does that mean?" There was silence, no answer at all. "I'm sorry," Hendricks said after a moment, composing himself. "What does Arch have to do with the end of the world?"

It took a while of listening to the line crackle before she finally spoke again. "Everything. He has everything to do with it." She sounded almost tender now, like she was delivering mortally bad news. Which, Hendricks supposed, she was.

"Archibald Stan is the man who will bring about the end of the world."

A Note to the Reader

If you enjoyed this book and want to know about future releases by Robert J. Crane, you can sign up for my NEW RELEASE EMAIL ALERTS! (You should also check out my other books. I've written kind of a lot of them.) I promise I won't spam you (I only send an email when I have a new book released) and I'll never sell your info. You can also unsubscribe at any time.

I also wanted to take a moment to thank you for reading this story. As an independent author, getting my name out to build an audience is one of the biggest priorities on any given day. If you enjoyed this story and are looking forward to reading more, let someone know - post it on Amazon, on your blog, if you have one, on Goodreads.com, place it in a quick Facebook status or Tweet with a link to the page of whatever outlet you purchased it from. Good reviews inspire people to take a chance on a new author – like me. And we new authors can use all the help we can get.

Thanks for reading.

Robert J. Crane

About the Author

Robert J. Crane was born and raised on Florida's Space Coast before moving to the upper midwest in search of cooler climates and more palatable beer. He graduated from the University of Central Florida with a degree in English Creative Writing. He worked for a year as a substitute teacher and worked in the financial services field for seven years while writing in his spare time. He makes his home in the Twin Cities area of Minnesota. Now he pretty much just sits around and writes books all day long.

He can be **contacted** in several ways:
Via email at cyrusdavidon@gmail.com
Follow him on Twitter – @robertJcrane
Connect on Facebook – robertJcrane (Author)
Website – http://www.robertJcrane.com
Blog – http://robertJcrane.blogspot.com
Become a fan on Goodreads – http://www.goodreads.com/RobertJCrane

Other Works by Robert J. Crane

The Sanctuary Series

Epic Fantasy

Defender: The Sanctuary Series, Volume One

Avenger: The Sanctuary Series, Volume Two

Champion: The Sanctuary Series, Volume Three

Crusader: The Sanctuary Series, Volume Four

Sanctuary Tales, Volume One - A Short Story Collection

Thy Father's Shadow: A Sanctuary Novel*

Master: The Sanctuary Series, Volume Five*

The Girl in the Box

Contemporary Urban Fantasy

Alone: The Girl in the Box, Book 1

Untouched: The Girl in the Box, Book 2

Soulless: The Girl in the Box, Book 3

Family: The Girl in the Box, Book 4

Omega: The Girl in the Box, Book 5

Broken: The Girl in the Box, Book 6

Enemies: The Girl in the Box, Book 7

Legacy: The Girl in the Box, Book 8

Destiny: The Girl in the Box, Book 9*

Power: The Girl in the Box, Book 10*

Southern Watch

Contemporary Urban Fantasy

Called: Southern Watch, Book 1

Depths: Southern Watch, Book 2*

* Forthcoming

38855591R00105

Made in the USA
Lexington, KY
12 May 2019